About the Author

Mikaila Lexie has always loved reading and writing, whether it be short poems or intricate stories. Being able to share her stories with others, while doing something she loves, is one that she could never replace or imagine erasing from her life.

Hearing people enjoy her work is one of her personal achievements that words can simply not describe, and she thanks each and every one that continues to support her.

Money, Deceit, and Pleasure

Mikaila Lexie

Money, Deceit, and Pleasure

Olympia Publishers
London

www.olympiapublishers.com
OLYMPIA PAPERBACK EDITION

Copyright © Mikaila Lexie 2024

The right of Mikaila Lexie to be identified as author of
this work has been asserted in accordance with sections 77 and 78 of
the Copyright, Designs and Patents Act 1988.

All Rights Reserved

No reproduction, copy or transmission of this publication
may be made without written permission.
No paragraph of this publication may be reproduced,
copied or transmitted save with the written permission of the publisher,
or in accordance with the provisions
of the Copyright Act 1956 (as amended).

Any person who commits any unauthorised act in relation to
this publication may be liable to criminal
prosecution and civil claims for damage.

A CIP catalogue record for this title is
available from the British Library.

ISBN: 978-1-80439-851-7

This is a work of fiction.
Names, characters, places and incidents originate from the writer's
imagination. Any resemblance to actual persons, living or dead, is
purely coincidental.

First Published in 2024

Olympia Publishers
Tallis House
2 Tallis Street
London
EC4Y 0AB

Printed in Great Britain

Dedication

I dedicate this book to my grandma, Dorothy. You always said I was a great writer, and I think of you with every accomplishment I reach as an author. Miss and love you always, Grandmama.

Acknowledgments

Thank you to all my people who do whatever they can to help support me throughout my journey. You are all appreciated and loved more than you will ever know.

Introduction

The darkest secrets within the world have always become a fascination of mine. From the depths of hell that lurk alongside twisted individuals onto the plea bargains for someone willing to take a life that's causing an inconvenience to another. One can remain afloat on top of it. You are born, you live, you work, and then you die. You remain completely oblivious to this situation on earth. Or you can dig deeper and request to be a part of something bigger. This grows to become a pattern, which leads to even more riches and bigger things, while sacrificing others. You see, there are really only two ways through it. To become a constant worker bee, or to become a queen bee and rule this bitch.

Chapter One

The funeral procession ended roughly about four o'clock and you could hear the last vehicle heading away from the cemetery and back down to civilization. Our town cemetery was about a twenty-minute drive up a windy road that was now totally devoted to strictly the cemetery. It once was a popular date night road that led high school bonfires or first-time hookup sessions, but a lot had changed since I was sixteen to now me being thirty-five.

I turned back toward my worker, Seth, and motioned him to finish dropping the dirt on the black casket that now lay six feet below ground level. He simply shot me a quick head nod and continued swinging and filling his bucket with soft brown dirt that would make a satisfying thud as it began to become piled on top of itself, while climbing higher and higher out of the hole.

I took a deep breath and titled my head from side to side before pulling my sunglasses off and placing them on top of my dark red hair. It was a beautiful day for a funeral, not too hot but warm and bright enough for sunglasses to cover the puffy tear-soaked eyes.

My name was Laylin Brown and I was the owner of Guardian Angels Funeral Home. Situated in my small hometown of roughly five thousand people. I had always dreamed of being a business woman but wasn't aware that it was going to be focused on owning my own funeral home. One day around the age of thirteen, I just became absolutely fascinated with the proceedings of end-of-life care. There was something about being the last person to take care of the human body. It was like a dance with the leftover skin and bone suit of some beautiful soul that was now flying high in the sky. It never disturbed me, it more so became like an art of preserving these bodies for the families to have their final moments of closure and peace before sending them to their final resting places.

Some of my close friends and family members seemed shocked to find out that I would be taking on the role of an embalmer and mortician, but they did nonetheless support me through my endeavors.

Life was absolutely blissful to me. I was a successful mortician in a small town where everyone knew basically everyone. There was the odd new face but everyone around here was friendly and always willing to help out or cheer someone on. I was very well loved and praised for the work I did for the community and families that I had known for so long. I was one of the most respected morticians around and I was the only one who owned a funeral home in this town. A population of five thousand wasn't big enough to commence two funeral home operations. Once opening mine five years ago, after taking over for the now-retired mortician and having nothing but great outcomes, the town kind of left me in charge of the whole dying business.

I watched Seth dump his last load of dirt and then start to smooth everything out nicely. Last thing to place was the headstone and then we would be able to pack up and head back to the funeral home. Today's proceedings was the only major thing on our to-do list, so an easy cleanup afternoon was in store for both of us. Followed, of course, by my final finishing touches of paperwork that was required by law.

"Great job, thanks, Seth." His feet hit the ground as his name left my mouth.

"Thanks, boss!" He smiled and then we both turned toward the Tahoe and began heading for it. Seth had been my worker for two years. He was twenty-three and a wonderful, hard, dedicated worker. He seemed to do more flirting than most of my other employees, but I came to find out fast that it was completely harmless. He was just a regular horny boy in his early twenties, that tried to flex his muscles to any damsel he could lay his eyes on.

Today had been a successful day and I felt the same sense of pride and accomplishment as I did every time a service went off without a hitch. We both made our way through the exit of the cemetery, while still en route to the work truck sitting in the parking lot. It would be a fabulous end to a day and a great relax, unwind day when I got home to kick my boots off and put my feet up!

Chapter Two

I tapped the unlock button on my keys a few times right before we reached the Tahoe doors. I reached my hand out and grabbed the smooth black diamond pearl paint handle and gave a gentle tug to swing my driver's door open. Seth proceeded to follow suit and climbed into my passenger seat.

I loved my work truck. It was my newly upgraded death care wagon that I knew I just had to correlate into my work. I respected and understood the hearses that were continuously and mostly used, but I was not into buying one, then leaving it parked out front of the funeral home. I loved the Tahoe option, it had four-wheel drive and sat up higher, so that you didn't have to awkwardly bend to try and lift a casket out of the back or put one in. It was completely black, topped with shiny black rims and tint just dark enough to see the figures in the front seat and completely blacked out on the back half so you couldn't see into the remainder of the vehicle. It was a little bit of a pricier investment but with the consistent pick-ups from the hospital, then hauling to services; it seemed to work better for my staff and I. It was also an added bonus that it was comfier and a rightfully beautiful unit.

I started the truck and slid it into gear and we began heading down the road and back toward town. The radio was playing a soft hum in the background as I watched the shadows of the trees go by, while I continued on driving through them.

Seth sat in the passenger seat, playing on his phone and

chewing on a piece of gum. We always got along good but usually after a service, we didn't talk or visit too much. We normally just sat in our own thoughts or he checked up on his social media or girlfriends. It always made me giggle at him to hear about his new-found social media fame or the new girl he thought wanted him. He was a character on his own for sure.

Twenty minutes had come and gone and I flipped my signal light on to make the left turn into the parking lot of the funeral home. I loved this building just as much as my work truck. It was a delicately sculpted and upgraded building, from its original old warehouse that it had been to a beautifully painted gray building with long tinted windows across the front. This allowed for the light to be let in for us on the inside but kept the nosey people from being able to look through and in from the outside. Our front door always remained locked, unless under special circumstances that it needed to be left open. Our guests were always buzzed in from a button that sits on my receptionist's desk and if someone was not seen, there was an outdoor doorbell that would allow them to ring it, so they could be brought in. This security measure was in place to help keep the upmost respect and privacy of the deceased and their grieving families.

I parked in the corner stall where the Tahoe always sat and shut off the engine. Seth and I both grabbed our things and climbed out and headed toward the front door. It was like held conditioned clock work and we both knew where we were going and what we were doing next. I held my key chip over the lock and pulled on the door handle to open it after hearing the slight buzz. The door was a bit heavy, so it took a good heave to get it swung open all the way.

Inside the door about twenty feet ahead sat my front

reception desk and my receptionist, Ayda. I had hired Ayda from the very beginning of me opening my doors. We were very close in age and she was a single, kid-less woman who loved her job and her social life. She was a petite blonde and had the most comforting and soothing voice that I had ever heard. She made everyone's transition from having a living relative to a deceased one, much easier. I was lucky enough to have her working for me and so appreciative of her. We shared a quick hello and I turned to the left to head toward my office, while Seth turned right to head back toward the lunch room, embalming rooms, viewing rooms, walk-in refrigerator, and showing room.

    I flicked on my light as I walked through the doorway of my office. I saw my computer was lit right up, which meant about a hundred emails that had been gathering and sitting there waiting for me. I rounded my huge c-shaped desk and plopped my stuff down on the corner of it before allowing myself to gently sit in my chair and roll up toward my computer. I leaned forward to remove my jacket and then swished my hair to my right shoulder before beginning to log in and look into my emails. I would check a few first to make sure there was nothing urgent and then continue on with finishing up my paperwork from today's service. It would then be filed away and the proper, required documents sent away that needed to be sent. I listened to my nails click the keys of my keyboard as I zoned out and into my computer screen and began to work.

Chapter Three

The ring of my office phone made me jump. I looked down to see it was Ayda calling from the front desk. Before I picked it up, I looked down to check on the time on my computer screen to see that it was already almost five thirty. I guess it wasn't bad, seeing as we didn't make it back to the funeral home until almost four forty-five.

"Hey, Laylin, sorry to bug you but there's a couple of officers here for you at the front desk. They are waiting to speak with you." Ayda's voice seemed normal and calm. Which, there was no reason that it shouldn't be. It wasn't the first time that we had police officers to show up here. It wasn't an everyday occurrence but it did happen occasionally. Mostly if they did show up, it was to discuss the state of one's body that came in from an abusive past, that way they could press the appropriate charges or for simply identifying missing persons.

"Okay, sounds good; let them know I'll be right there. Thanks, Ayda!" I pushed myself back from my desk and stood up. I tugged the tops of my pants that had begun riding up from sitting and started to head toward my door. I decided today I would wear nice chunky heels, with nice black high waist relaxed fit pants, topped with a pink business tank top, finished with my black watch. My deep red hair lay curled and bounced softly up and down as I took each stride. These were my casual business clothes and the most comfy. I always loved the deep tones of my red hair because it always seemed to top each outfit perfectly.

It didn't take me long before I reached the last corner and as I rounded it, I could see the two cops standing beside one another looking around at different things that were laid out in the front of the reception area. I walked straight up to them and stuck out my hand to greet them both.

"Hello, gentlemen, my name is Laylin Brown, I am the owner." I ended my statement with a professional smile as I shook each one of their hands.

"Nice to meet you, Laylin. I'm Glen Crot, and this is my partner, Dave Frule." The partner nodded his head as he was introduced by Glen. I usually knew almost all of the police force, especially since owning Guardian Angels Funeral Home, but these two gentlemen I had never come into contact enough even for a simple introduction before just now.

"What can I help y'all with today?" I clasped my hands together and placed them in front of me while waiting for their reply.

"We have a family that would like their deceased family member to be exhumed for reevaluation." The statement caught me off guard. In all my years of school, and working under someone and then owning my own funeral home, I had never had someone from the family request an exhumation. It just wasn't a typical week for a mortician. Usually, everything was done prior, so that this type of thing wasn't done mainly for the costs associated with it but also because of the body decay that would begin to happen after a lengthy time of sitting in a sealed box underground. Exhumations were done and requested, but again it was so rare for it to be requested from the family members themselves.

"Wow." This was beginning to turn into a conversation that

I didn't think my receptionist needed to hear or anyone else if they came walking into the reception area.

"Are you able to follow me into my office and we finish talking there?" Both Glen and Dave nodded and I turned and started to head back to my office. I could hear the footsteps of the officers behind me following closely and quietly. When I hit my door, I stepped off to the side and held my hand out to escort them in and toward the two leather chairs sitting on the opposite side of my desk. Glen was the second one through and I followed in behind him, shutting the door with my foot before rounding my desk and taking a seat myself.

"And the purposes for the exhumation are for investigation purposes?" I had the right to ask these questions pertaining to an exhumation. If they were here, it was because my workers and my business was the one that got the body ready and laid it to rest. Or else it was still registered through us from the old funeral home and workers that we had taken over for and replaced.

"The family believes there were things that were not supposed to be buried and the cause of death was faulty and wrong." Both Dave and Glen had the look of disgust strewn across their faces. I didn't blame them, there was something a little eerie about bringing back up the dead and digging around in their casket.

"Okay. The family, they do know what the costs are that are associated with this and the legal paperwork to fill out, as well as the emotional trauma that it can ensue from seeing a decaying family member's body? Especially because it will need to be re-examined and another autopsy performed to reevaluate the body." They both looked pale but slowly nodded. I titled my head to the side and raised my eyebrows as I released a slight sigh before continuing onward.

"Okay then. This will take a few days to get sorted out, a few months to wait for approval and paperwork signed and filed. I will print the forms for you two and then I will print the forms for the family and make an appointment with them to come in and finalize things with me. Can I get the name of the deceased that we will be exhuming, please?" Glen leaned over slightly in his chair to grab a little notebook out of his pocket.

"Cristina Waytes." I clicked my mouse to exit out of my emails and went into the database to search up Cristina Waytes' name. I needed to see what plot she was in, if she had actually been buried and not cremated and the family wasn't just losing their minds. I also needed to know when she had died and what the cause of her death was determined to be.

Both gentlemen sat very quietly watching me type and scroll on my computer. Lots of people always felt pressure when they had an audience watching and waiting to hear from them but this never seemed to faze or bother me.

I scrolled through the "c" column until I found her name. I clicked on it so that I could pull up all of her details in her case file.

"Okay, I have it here. So, she was nineteen, born February 2, 1985, died August 19, 2004, is that correct?" I had to make sure that their dates lined up with mine so that I wasn't sharing someone else's confidential information. I only had one Cristina Waytes in my system but that didn't mean that there weren't others out in the world, so it still could be a chance that my Cristina Waytes was different from theirs.

"Yes, that's her date of birth and the day she died." The feeling in my gut turned into uncertainty for a moment. Why after all this time would the family feel that they needed to exhume their daughter's body? I could only imagine it was her parents doing it, but why? It had been seventeen years. I could already smell the casket before it was even dug up and uncovered. I had been around for some grave site diggings and have come across old caskets that were accidentally dug up. It was never a pretty scene and the smell; well, that's something so unforgettable that you really want to be able to forget about it but you just can't. A staining of your memory as well as a total remembering recognition for your nose hairs. I cleared my throat before proceeding forward.

"Perfect. I will print this page off and get all the forms that I need printed off for you guys and then I'll be able to send you on your way." They both silently nodded and agreed. I really couldn't blame them; mortician and funeral home work wasn't really for the faint of heart, especially when it came to talking about prodding into a decaying corpse's casket.

My printer spit out the last few pages that the cops would need to take back and fill out for their legal requirements. I needed at least one cop to be around when the exhumation happened. They never wanted to do it but it was a legal requirement of mine. I grabbed my stapler and tapped all my papers on my desk so they would align perfectly before stapling them together. I handed it over across my desk toward Glen, after they had all been fastened together.

"Everything you guys need to fill out is there and if you have any questions, please feel free to call me. I always have my cell with me. It is linked to my number if it is afterhours and you call the funeral home number, it will come to my phone. I just ask that you leave the family's name and number here with me so that I can schedule a meeting and get them in here to finalize their end of the paperwork." Glen reached out and took the paperwork from my hand before beginning his reply.

"No problem. I will write it down and leave it for you and we will get this finished up and either faxed or dropped back off with you." He took a pen out of his shirt pocket and opened a new page in his notebook, then began scribbling down the name and number. He licked his thumb and reached down to rip off the page he had just written on. I reached my hand out and grabbed it, while sending a nod toward the both of them.

"Thank you very much, gentlemen." I pushed my chair back to stand up and they started to shuffle out of their seats.

"Yes, thank you, Laylin. We will be in touch." I met their hands for another quick goodbye handshake and followed them to my door. They opened my door and started to head back toward the main entrance. I turned around to head back to my desk to get things tidied up, finished and shut down so that I could head home.

My hands felt sweaty, so I wiped them gently on my pants before snapping my fingers and bending over my computer to power it down. The curiosity became to loom inside of me and the million questions started to surface. What the hell were these people looking for?

Chapter Four

I had a ton of thoughts still twisting through my brain as to why someone would want to dig up their loved one after so many years. She was only nineteen when she passed, so again my bet was that it was her parents that wanted the exhumation to take place. There wouldn't even be anything but bones and slop. Not literal slop, it's just what I called it. All the body decay and ground water that seeped into the casket that lay underground alongside the body all these years. I really couldn't even figure out what they were thinking that they would find. If there was some sort of small possession, they would literally have to wait until the casket was drained before finding it, unless of course it was able to float.

I finished staring off into the distance of my office corner and looked down at my watch to see it was now six-thirty. Half an hour past closing and everyone would already be gone. I was ready for the ending to my day as well. The thought of bourbon on ice tempted my thoughts and it seemed like a fitting way to finish off my day. A new task to adhere to as soon as I made it home. I grabbed my jacket and swung it up and down onto my arms before bending down to grab my bag and keys. I headed out of my office and swung the door shut behind me as I exited.

I never had to worry about shutting off any lights or locking any doors, all our main doors locked behind you and the lights in the building were set to be turned off from nine at night to six in the morning. If there was a body that needed to be brought in between those hours, you simply just went to the side of the reception area and turned them on. Otherwise, I had a system on my phone that enabled me to turn them on before I even entered the building.

I walked past the front of the building in the direction of my personal vehicle. I had already hit my command start on my escalade and I could hear the sweet rumble of it idling in my parking stall about eighty feet away. There was something to be said about my vehicle style. Like my work Tahoe, my Cadillac was in the same scheme of blacked out rims and tinted windows but the body paint was instead pearl diamond white. It was another beautiful unit I was proud of, definitely another costly investment but I never had to worry about fuel or space because it was a beast in both categories.

I grabbed my door handle and lifted my stuff in first before climbing in behind it. My phone reconnected and my music started to play. Ahh! I loved this song! The words were always pulsing with beautiful poetry but the beat of the music was one that sung straight to your soul. Being able to take my twenty-minute drive home, decompress and listen to my music was one of my favorite times of the day.

I threw my truck into reverse and cranked my tunes before starting to back out. Now to get home and have that glass of bourbon before tomorrow's day's daunting task of getting in touch and involved with a distraught family.

Maybe they weren't distraught and I was thinking too much into it. Just get home and enjoy yourself and take tomorrow as it comes, no need to panic or stress about the unknowns before they even happen. It makes no sense and only sends panic where there is no panic. My little inner voice was such a superstar some days. I honestly never really disagreed with it and even if I did, the occasion seemed to be rare.

Ten more minutes left until I turned into my driveway, music blasting, sun shining, and the bliss of the uncomplicated little things.

Chapter Five

I rolled into the parking lot and backed into my parking stall. Today's morning was absolutely gorgeous, going to be a nice eighteen or nineteen plus day outside, accompanied by a small breeze. These were the absolute best days in my opinion.

I walked over to the front door and put my chip up to the doors to unlock it and swing it open. I gently swung it open and hustled in before it closed shut behind me. It was now ten after ten and I needed to get settled in so I could make the phone call to Cristina Waytes' family.

Ayda was already here, perched behind the reception desk. We opened at ten but she was always here about a half an hour early to make sure everything was tidied up and she had all her tasks for the day lined up and ready to go.

"How's it going today, beautiful?" Ayda's welcomes were always so warm and welcoming. Even on the rough mornings she always knew how to make a person feel good; become a little lighter and more cheery.

"Absolutely wonderful so far! And you? You have a good evening and such?" Ayda lit up and she shared how her niece was now starting to babble words and walk. She only ever boasted about her niece and when other kids were brought into the conversation, Ayda would always let the conversation go flat or simply die. No one was more important to her than her niece, Maya.

We finished our small talk before I ended it and began to

make the walk back to my office. I began to feel a little unsettled again once I began to think about what was bound to go on and how all of this would play out with this exhumation. It really wasn't up to me to decide on if a family was able to handle it or not. I just had to be the funeral service that dug their deceased's family member's body out of the ground and brought it back up to the surface.

Now this was a very intriguing scenario for me, too. I personally had not been the mortician to work on Cristina or even bury her. This was before my time as even being an apprentice or finishing my schooling. I had only been in practice in the industry for ten years and this girl had been deceased now for seventeen years. The only reason that I had the records of where she lay to rest, how she was pronounced dead, and the name of the mortician who worked on her and when she was worked on, was because it was from the old mortician that I had taken over for in my small town. Therefore, all the previous records just slid into my own database that was registered for our town cemetery. It also kept the records for up to fifty years for various reasons, this being one of them.

It was mostly used in investigating cases or just seeing and acknowledging the state one's body was in or how their body was handled, either by cremation or buried. It was all a very neat system and I was always kept intrigued by seeing how the paperwork aspect and the handling of bodies went. Guess that's what you needed to be able to be in this line of work, consistently intrigued.

I opened my paperwork and saw the name and number of the family member to Christina Waytes. It was her mother. Her name was Lydia and her phone number was only a few digits off of the funeral homes, which usually meant she probably lived pretty close to the funeral home.

I took a quick sip of my coffee from my tumbler before picking up my office phone and starting to dial her phone number. This was always the waiting game part. To see how people were going to react and their understanding. Also, how I handle them and how to communicate with them delicately, in their sensitive time and situation. It was one of the basics taught in school and one that I seemed to be very good with.

The phone started to ring and I cleared my throat softly, so I would have a crisp and clear voice, while introducing myself. It only took two rings before I heard the other line pick up.

"Hello?" It was a woman's voice and I could only assume it was Lydia that I had connected with.

"Hello, this is Laylin Brown calling from Guardian Angels Funeral Home. May I speak with Lydia Waytes, please?" There was a quiet pause and I knew that at these moments, I had to be patient and not to become impatient. It only took maybe thirty seconds before the woman started to speak.

"Yes, this is she."

"Hi, Lydia. So, I was informed yesterday that you want to proceed forward with an exhumation for your daughter Cristina Waytes. So, what we need to do to move forward is I need to set up a meeting with you, whenever you are wanting and able. I have to get paperwork filled out and filed, as well as I would like to meet you in person to discuss your desires and expectations from the exhumation. Is there a time when you are able or do you have any questions you would like to ask me?"

Lydia's sudden response took me by surprise. I figured she would need to take a few moments the first time I explained everything to her.

"I don't have any questions for you to answer for me. Does today around one work for you to set up a meeting?"

I quickly pulled up my calendar and saw that nothing was

booked other than of course the possible walk ins that came occasionally.

"Sure! That will work perfectly for me. And do you know where we are located?" Seemed like such a silly question for me to be asking, but I always had to just for the chances that they did not actually know where we were situated in this town.

"Yes, I do." Lydia seemed prompt but not at all rude. I kind of enjoyed the style; it was a change from the usual.

"Okay, wonderful. So please note that our front doors do remain locked but once you get here if you aren't let in within a few minutes, please ring the doorbell on the left-hand side and someone will let you in shortly thereafter."

"Okay, thank you, Laylin." I felt a sense of relief wash over me as I was starting to believe that maybe this would be a level-headed meeting and exhumation.

"No problem. I will see you at one!" I heard the phone disconnect and the dead tone start to echo in my ear. She was most definitely prompt. The quick phone hang up made me giggle as I put the phone back down on its holder. A woman who knew what she wanted and how to precisely make plans without beating around the bush. Maybe Lydia and I would get along great and our meeting to get to the exhumation process would be done quickly and smoothly.

I grabbed my coffee and took another swig before tilting my head back and forth. I then picked up my hands to start typing on my keyboard to see what emails were sitting and waiting for me. Three more hours to go and the interesting part of my day would begin.

Chapter Six

I only had the three hours before Lydia would be coming in to meet with me. I didn't have anything scheduled other than our staff's weekly meeting at eleven. This usually took about an hour for us all and was mostly just to talk about the upcoming events, how things were going, if supplies were needing to be ordered, if things didn't go very well the previous week and where we could improve. I always loved these meetings, not only did it let my staff and I, all get on the exact page for the week but it also seemed like an hour break away from the craziness or the sadness that loomed from a busy week.

In total, I have six employees who work here, this includes myself as well. Yes, I was the owner but I also was the main funeral director, along with sometimes doing the odd embalming, if I wanted to or needed to. Ayda was always my receptionist and that's how she preferred along with all that she wanted to be involved with, in the funeral home. Seth was my helper. He did funerals, dug graves, performed exhumations and transported bodies from where they were temporarily being housed, back to the funeral home. Chloe was one of my embalmers, she only did embalming. Gregory was another embalmer; he as well only did embalming. Both of Chloe and Gregory's work was impeccable and they were highly requested embalmers. This not only made me proud but made my funeral home stand out wonderfully. Tristan was my cremator; he did only cremations and did them very proficiently.

The crematorium was located about one hundred feet from behind the main building. I decided to choose this design to minimize the noise and the smoke, along with the smell. Smell did travel outside and around the building, it did unfortunately stand out but once the smoke started to escape the pipe, it helped muffle the smell a bit. We had multiple filters along the stovepipe leading outside as well, which helped with masking the scent that was put off from burning dead bodies. We tried to avoid cremations during our busiest times with family meetings, but sometimes it was just unavoidable. The funeral home itself wasn't located directly in town so it wasn't a horror sight to a busy street to see the chimney pouring out smoke and knowing that bodies were being burned.

Sometimes, we had a few more employees who joined us, sometimes helpers in the busiest of times or a new student that needed placement or sponsorship to receive their diploma for funeral services. These were both rare situations because most students went to higher population areas for schooling and we were never overly busy.

In this industry, it always remained pretty much steady, with the occasional pickup in business. With my small numbered staff, I was able to pay them great wages, keep them steady with work, as well as there was almost no drama between anyone and we were all able to maintain a good balance between work and our social lives. This didn't include me, though, of course. Funerals were held on any given day that a family chose, as well as phone calls for new intakes did come at any time of the day no matter what the day. I really didn't mind though, I wasn't married; I didn't have any kids or even an animal at home waiting for me. It was solely me, my job and this business was my partner and baby. I actually kind of preferred it that way.

My staff would only be called in when needed but we did have a spacious walk-in refrigerator. This was amazing because when bodies were brought in, they didn't need to be flushed and pumped with formaldehyde right away to slow down the beginning stages of decomposition. We were never overloaded and the bodies that we had for a few days, would be moved out and be buried or cremated just as fast as new bodies were being brought in. It seemed that with everything working together in perfect union, I was able to operate a proficient, sanitary, well-respected funeral home within the hours of ten a.m. to six p.m., Monday through Friday, excluding the services that were scheduled and carried through outside of our normal operating times.

My funeral home and workers seemed to be a big success along with valued, and a sense of pride was always followed by every successful funeral or viewing that we accomplished.

Chapter Seven

"Thanks, guys." I smiled and turned to head out of the meeting room. I looked down at my watch to see it was already almost twelve-thirty and my one o'clock appointment would be here shortly. Well, today, it was going to be a fast protein shake day because I didn't have time to make some extraordinary cuisine or run out and pick something up for lunch.

We did have a staff kitchen and lunch room, but I had a little mini fridge in my office where I liked to keep my lunch. It made it quicker to access and I lost less time getting myself food when I was having a full and busy day that consisted of meetings, phone calls, or organizing funeral processions.

I shut my door as I walked in so I could have a few quiet minutes to myself before the rest of the day would become filled with important discussions and finalizing dates. I grabbed a bottle of protein shake from the bottom left corner and gave it a few shakes to mix up whatever had settled onto the bottom. I peeled the wrapper and heard the plastic snap as I turned the cap to break the seal and open it. I took a long big swig and felt the strawberry banana shake run down my throat. Man, I loved these things; they were like crack to me. This little gas station on the corner lot in town had them and I always bought five or six each time I visited it. Just so I could restock the fridge in my office for moments exactly like this one.

I spun my chair back around to face my computer and bent down to my drawer to gather the paperwork that I would need filled out and the paperwork needed for Lydia about the proceedings of her daughter's exhumation. There was tons of paperwork when it came to exhumations. It wasn't just an easy thing to pull a decomposed or decaying body out of the ground that was already put to rest. It always turned into quite the affair but everyone had their reasons and I was not the one to judge. In the world we lived in, it was honestly one of the least odd things to want to do with a decomposing body.

I had just gathered a few pens and started to tuck my hair behind my ear when I heard my office phone start to ring. I looked down and saw the call was coming from Ayda at reception.

"Hi, Ayda." My answer was prominent because I already knew why she was calling me.

"Laylin, a Lydia Waytes is here for your one o'clock appointment."

"Please bring her to my office." I hung up and pushed my chair back so I could stand up and start toward the door to open it for her. I always found it more welcoming to clients when I was the one to open my door and welcome them into my office. It seemed more personable than staying seated behind my desk and waiting for them to walk in.

It didn't take long and I could see Ayda's shadow along the hallway wall as I swung my office door open. I stepped back as I saw Ayda appear in my doorway. She stepped off to the side and a small petite woman in her fifties stopped in my doorway. I offered a small smile and moved my hand to gesture her in, while still holding onto my door handle. She stepped through without making a single noise or having an expression crease her face. I gave a quick nod to Ayda before starting to shut the door quickly and quietly. I turned around to find Lydia standing by my two guest office chairs, awaiting instruction.

"Please have a seat, Lydia." I finished her name with a smile on my lips and a soft gentle tone for the landing of my directions. She grabbed the nearest chair and seated herself firmly. I walked around my desk and slid my chair under my butt before sitting down and sliding the last way up to my desk. I looked down at my paperwork as I touched the tops of the pages and then I picked up my head to look up at Lydia. She was staring at me with this distant look on her face. I couldn't quite pinpoint what it meant, but it kind of made me feel awkward and a little out of place in my own office.

"Thank you for coming in and meeting with me today. I'm Laylin and it is very nice to meet you, sorry for the circumstances that we are having to meet under." Lydia closed her eyes and gave one simple nod down before clasping her hands and picking her head back up to look me in my eyes.

"Shall we begin?" I sat quiet for a moment wondering if it would take her a minute to say yes. Sometimes people needed their time and there was never any rushing from me during such heartbreaking times.

"Yes." Lydia's reply came so quick and prompt it almost made me jump from being startled and caught off guard. I cleared my throat and grabbed my pen before settling my hands comfortably on my desk and replacing my gaze back on Lydia. This was going to be an interesting meeting, I already could feel it.

Chapter Eight

"There are a bunch of questions that I will need to ask regarding the exhumation. These questions will need to be diligently listened to and answered as honestly and to the best of your ability as possible. Everything will be noted and written down to be kept within the records of the state and the funeral home, as well as with your family and of course your daughters records Cristina Waytes. Some of the things that I have to ask, may be personal and hard to hear, therefore please take your time in answering and if we need to come back to the question, we most certainly can. Does everything make sense and do you understand all that I have laid out and explained?"

Lydia silently nodded and I could hear her swallow come across almost as a gulp. I never wanted to make people feel afraid of the questions but especially when it came to exhumations, a lot of information was needed answered and recorded for not only the sake of the funeral home and the family of the deceased but also for the legality reasonings behind it.

Lydia's face seemed to become a little paler than when she first arrived in my office and I figured this would be the time to offer her something to drink before we started a lengthy meeting about her dead daughter.

"Lydia, can I get you anything to drink? Water, tea, coffee? Maybe some juice or pop?" She looked as though she was going to reject but then she shifted in her seat and cleared her throat before answering.

"I'll have a water, please."

I smiled and gave her a quick nod before turning my chair to the side and reaching down into my fridge to grab her a new bottle. We had our own waters from the funeral home and we willingly gave them out to whoever and whenever. Even when someone declined, we still tried to encourage them to take one with them just in case they felt like they needed a drink to avoid puking or fainting. The in-depth details about someone's recently passed loved one, usually brought upon one or both of those responses.

I closed the fridge door while I spun back around to be fully facing Lydia and handed her water toward her and placed it down beside her arm.

"Are you ready to begin?" Lydia shot back a nod, so I picked up my first page and settled it straight down in front of me and picked up my pen.

"So today is February 26, 2021, and we are here today to write down the details and fill in the blanks as to why you are wanting or needing to pursue an exhumation of the deceased, Cristina Waytes. She was nineteen years old when she passed and it was concluded at the time of her passing that she had been killed in a car accident." I paused my readings to look up at Lydia to make sure what I had already said wasn't sitting wrong or deemed false. She was slowly nodding her head with an expressionless look on her face. I cleared my throat before beginning again.

"Cristina's body was still intact when brought in and transferred from the hospital and a regular embalming session and body cleanup, along with the regular standard getting ready for viewing, was performed before the family had the viewing and finalized plans for the funeral. She was laid to rest Sunday August 3, 2004 and had an open casket service. She was buried in the graveyard of Hope Spencerville at approximately four p.m. in the afternoon." I finished my sentence before reaching over to grab my own water and have a quick drink. Though it never really bothered me to do my regular proceedings, there was something about exhumation appointments that seemed to leave a little hole in my heart. Maybe it was because it was like cutting open an old scar that eventually healed and pouring a little salt in it for another burn around the clock.

I could understand the different reasonings as in why people would want to bring family members bodies back up or why sometimes they had to come back up for a more in-depth investigation or a newly found clue in an investigation. What I couldn't understand was why a family would want to stand by and actually witness us pulling their loved one from their peaceful resting place after the decomposition stages had almost fully eaten away at what we remembered them as and only left a pile of slimy bodily fluids and bones.

The silence in my office was overtaking and I decided to finish everything that I needed to present so maybe it would break the ice or possibly speed the process up.

"I will need to know when you would like the exhumation to take place. Please be advised though that it can take upwards of three months to receive the okay and approval of a requested exhumation. I will need to know the amount of people who will be attending with you, if any and we will need to arrange the day, so at least two police officers are able to be there and attend. Along with us, the funeral home, you and your family, the police need to have a witness and signing off officers to make sure that the exhumation process was done to legal standards. Does this make sense?"

"Yes, it all makes sense and I understand everything completely. Thank you for helping me with this. I'd like to have the exhumation done as quickly as we can so we can leave Cristina to rest again and not have to disturb her anymore. You see the reasoning for all of this, we received a package in the mail last week. It didn't have a return address and was just marked to 'Cristina Waytes Family.' We were intrigued but also disturbed especially at the fact that it has been so long. We eventually opened it and saw that it contained a broach that was put into her casket with her, on the day she laid to rest. It was a passed down family broach, it was the one and only broach of its kind. No one but our family had known it existed and it wasn't even put into her casket until everyone else was gone, just before it was closed and lowered into the ground. Now, it has magically appeared from someone and placed into our mailbox. So now, I would like answers as to what the hell is going on. Was there actually a replica and someone is just messing with us? Or was it stolen from her casket before they piled dirt on top of her? I want to know and I have a damn well right to know." My stomach lurched at the end of Lydia's sentence. I felt sick to my core.

What kind of game was this, if it was someone messing with them? In all my years of working in funeral services, I had never heard of this and it was becoming increasingly more disturbing to me as the seconds raced by. I started to feel urges of anger and sadness along with Lydia and her family. Hell, I didn't even know what to say to her to help her feel more relaxed or calm about the whole situation or exhumation, or what was going on. I simply had no answers.

I grabbed my bottle for another slow drink of water before I could muster up the most delicate and respectful reply I could conjure.

"I'm so very sorry and saddened to hear the events that have led up to wanting to move forward with an exhumation. I can also understand the anger and confusion following it and why you are requesting and wanting this dealt with in a timely and efficient matter. Please know that I have nothing holding this back and will get this set up for you and your family as soon as possible. Then I hope that it can bring you all some comfort and peace back rather than back to the grief and passing of your daughter. This deeply saddens me, of the indescribable and unfortunate events brought upon you by someone else." I watched one single tear fall down Lydia's cheek as she gently bowed her head toward me. I passed a paper her way and placed a pen down gently toward her.

"All I need is your signature authorizing us to begin all the steps needed to move forward with this. After that we are all set and finished today, unless there's something else, I can help with or questions that I can answer for you. If there is not, I will finish up all the paperwork and call and arrange the setup for the exhumation, if and when it's approved, before calling to let you know which days are available and work for you." All Lydia seemed she could do was nod as she picked up the pen and started to scribble her signature.

She seemed like such a sweet, kind-hearted woman and it broke me to watch her relive the pain, sickening memories and thoughts of when her baby died at only nineteen years young. Life was cruel and unfair and the people living in it, well some were straight fucked within their heads. Especially ones that thought this was some sort of joke or whatever they thought it was. How someone could do this to a family or other human being was beyond me and I couldn't even try to fathom wrapping my brain around it.

After she finished signing, Lydia placed the pen down and grabbed the water bottle off of my desk. She stood up and I followed suit. I walked around my desk and went to open the door for her so she would be able to exit without having to pause to open it. When she reached the doorway, she stopped to look at me and reached her hand out toward me waiting for a hand shake. I gently reached out and grabbed her hand and gave it a few soft shakes with a smile.

"Thank you, Laylin, for being so helpful with this. I appreciate you taking the time to not only help with it but treat it as though I am an actual person and not just a business deal." I reached my second hand up to hold her hand in both of mine and gave it a squeeze.

"Thank you for entrusting me to help you with this and I hope we can give you some sort of answers that you are needing and looking for. I will be in touch and we will talk soon. It was nice meeting you, Lydia." She gave me one last smile before our hands broke apart and she started on down the hallway to exit the building. I started to head back toward my desk, shaking my head.

What a sick and messed up world to replicate something someone was buried with, or even worse, steal a family broach from a dead girl's casket and body before she was sealed and buried underground.

Chapter Nine

Three Months Later

The months passed quickly and with a few random calls from Lydia checking in to see if I'd heard anything back about the exhumation being a go, work and funeral processions continued on without hiccup or interruption. It was exactly three months to the day when my office phone rang and it was someone from the government telling me that Cristina Waytes exhumation was approved under special circumstances. Rather than having to unbury, exhume and haul back to the funeral home, we were being granted approval to do the extraction and retrieval right in the cemetery grounds as long as it was shut down and no onlookers were around and present. It was an odd expression but saved us much more time and I was thankful nonetheless.

"Thanks so much! I'll call Lydia right after we are done on the phone and let her know that tomorrow will work for everyone to go ahead with the exhumation at ten o'clock in the morning." With the ending of my sentence, I heard a quick "perfect" response followed by a thank you and then a clicking of the end of the phone call. I pulled my hair back and twisted it downward before letting it fall on my right collarbone. I let a heavy sigh leave my throat as I leaned back into my chair to relax for a few seconds. The day was already half over but it had already drained me like I had been here for more than fifteen hours.

Why was this hitting me so hard? Why was it sitting as so

disturbing, but so intriguing? Was it the story behind it, or the straight fact that we would be fishing for items along with bones throughout bodily fluids and ground water? Years after years in the ground didn't leave anything too pretty and when it came to bodies that always eventually decompose to nothing, the silt, slime and dirty water that held the bones and long loved possessions, became one of the most disturbing of liquids.

    I understood, I knew exactly why Lydia was moving forward and proceeding with an exhumation. It was to help clear a new set found of hurdles that had just been thrown their way after just grieving the first massive hurdle that life had thrown at them. I never did fully understand life in itself. It was always so complex, complicated, followed by blissful beautiful moments that were so gorgeous and magnificent that they would take your literal breath away. It was truly a remarkable, heart breaking and fascinating adventure that we all had, solely uniquely from one person to the next person. The chaos-mixed storm that circles and embellishes into love, was just one that no one could ever fully explain to its entirety.

    I picked up my water bottle and took three big chugs before closing the lid and placing it back down into its spot on my desk. Tomorrow at ten o'clock, if it worked for Lydia, we would be pulling her daughter out of the ground and sorting through it like alphabet soup. For some reason, besides the unpleasant feelings, it was running about as smoothly as it possibly could be. There was no hesitancy or drama issues that had arose yet and it seemed as though the whole exhumation process would run smoothly from start to finish, making this into maybe a week-long process rather than a few months long. This, I couldn't even be bored or frustrated with because a week timeline for an exhumation was almost deemed a miracle.

    I reached down to grab my office phone and picked it up

and started to dial the numbers of Lydia's phone number. It didn't even hit three rings before she picked up the phone.

"Hello, Lydia, it is Laylin calling. I have some news that we can carry onward with the exhumation of Cristina's resting place tomorrow starting at ten o'clock in the morning if that works for you?"

"Yes, that will work greatly. I will meet you at the cemetery tomorrow." The zero hesitancy in her reply helped with my assumptions that this was going to be a very fast flowing exhumation.

"Okay, perfect. It will be a longer process, we do not start until a little after ten, once everyone has gathered. The unburying, followed by the rest of our process and protocol does become lengthy for the day. So, please be aware that it will be more of a day long occurrence rather than a couple hours. I just like to make sure you're as prepared as you possibly can be during this difficult time." I could hear a faint sniffle come from beyond the phone before I heard Lydia clear her throat before beginning to reply to my testament.

"That is fine, I have nowhere else to be or rush to." I felt a ball form in my throat and some tears threaten my eyes. I wasn't a mother but I could only imagine the unimaginable feelings a mother would be having, listening to a conversation like this and then proceeding with the actions that were to come tomorrow.

"Okay. Thank you Lydia and we will all see you tomorrow at ten at the cemetery." I heard her almost whisper her goodbye before the line went dead.

I almost rarely got goodbyes, it always seemed as though when I was done, the phone was always just hung up or simply dropped from the news coming from my lips. This never bothered me, nor did I take it personally. I was dealing with people's hardest times in life and any reaction was acceptable to me. There was no right or wrong and there was definitely no area or room for me to feel offended by ones grieving actions. It was simply never about me.

My phone hung up with a smooth click as I laid it back in its holder. I looked down at my clock to see it was only four thirty. I flipped open my email, to see if there was any urgent emails or messages and then looked back at my phone to see if there were any messages waiting from the front desk. Nothing popped up as urgent, so I logged out of everything and sat back to close my eyes and take some deep breaths. Tomorrow was going to be exhausting. No matter how smoothly this was going to run, it would be emotionally exhausting. I opened my eyes back up and leaned forward to gather my things. I was going to head home and get a head start on my evening. Take a few extra hours for myself, for tomorrow was going to be one of the rougher ones for this month. I pushed my chair back as I stood up and headed out of my office toward the front reception area.

"I'm heading home early, Ayda, if it's an emergency direct it to my phone but if not just leave me a message and I'll get it tomorrow when I get back in from the exhumation. Have a good night, girly."

"Have a good night, Laylin." I lifted my hand in the air as I continued on to push the front doors open. I could hear my heels clicking across the pavement and I listened to the solitude it brought with a soft blowing breeze and fresh air. I listened to my keys rattle as I picked them up to hit the unlock button to my vehicle.

It was time to get in and blast my music and enjoy the simplicity of my evening and moments right now. Knowing when tomorrow came, it would be less than a comforting feeling and more of a whirlwind.

Chapter Ten

It was another beautiful day as I turned the truck onto the last corner before the "Road Closed" barricades and a cop car came into sight. This was part of our regular proceedings with an exhumation, with the exception of not having to move the casket back to the funeral home. There were no scheduled funeral processions for today, therefore the road to the cemetery would be blocked off except for the workers accompanying, the family and the police officers. One would stay down by the barricades to keep visitors out and the other would be up in the cemetery with everyone to make sure everything ran smoothly and went off without a hiccup.

As I got closer to the cop car, I could see it was Harold who was standing beside the hood of the car awaiting my Tahoe to make its full approach of where he stood. I started to roll my window down just before the front of my hood was equal with one of the barricades and came to a smooth and slow stop.

"Hey, Laylin, how's it going today?"

"Morning, Harold. Well, it's a beautiful day so cannot complain about that. Makes it a little easier to be outside for an exhumation when it's not pouring rain or freezing outside." I smiled as I finished my last word.

"Ain't that the truth. I already allowed Lydia in, as well as Conner is up there already and I see you have your worker with you as well." Harold gave a quick nod to Seth sitting in my passenger seat. Seth replied with a silent quick wave and continued to wait patiently before we continued heading up.

"I'll move the barricade for you and you guys can head on up."

"Thanks, Harold." I nodded and smiled before he turned around to grab the barricade and slide it out of my way. I let my brake release and eased my Tahoe up the last stretch just before coming to the cemetery's parking lot. I could see Lydia's vehicle parked off to the left side of Conner's patrol car and I drove over to the right side to pull into the closest stall to the gate entering the grounds.

Seth was here to operate the hoe and exhume the casket from the ground. He did a great job always; he wasn't only a smooth operator but he was also efficient and fast. In funeral times, that made life a little easier to navigate, watching smooth transitions, rather than jerky horrible movements. This young guy was definitely a great attribute to me and the funeral home.

I grabbed my coffee mug and shut the Tahoe off while gathering my phone and keys. I looked over to see Seth picking up his water and phone.

"You ready to start this day?"

He looked over at me and nodded. We grabbed our door handles and both stepped out. Seth hit the ground first and I heard his door shut as I straightened out my black dress. I turned to the side to grab my door and swung it shut before hitting the lock button. We would be the only ones up here, but it was always a habit to lock the work vehicle because there was always some sort of confidential paperwork, items, or bodies sitting inside of it.

I bent down to fix the back of my wedge before starting toward the gate to let myself into the cemetery. I always dressed business and professional like, even on the days when there would be more manual labor than anything. This was my business and I was always in charge of not only handling the paperwork end but also being there for families that were having to be a part of such hardship times. It always seemed to go better with a well-dressed and smelling person, or so I thought anyway.

I saw a puff of smoke and heard the hoe fire up and knew Seth was already on it. As I walked through the gate, I could see Lydia standing with Conner over beside her daughter's grave. It was off to the back left of the graveyard and on the outside of a row. That was extremely convenient, Seth wouldn't have to be weaving through headstones and trying to avoid wrecking the expensive granite that lay decorating the occupied gravesites. I could feel the stillness within the air before I even reached both Lydia and Conner. Yeah, today was definitely going to be a hard one.

I thought Lydia was bringing someone with her? The inquisitive question popped into my brain before I whisked it away. It was truly none of my business and really who would want to see the remnants of what's left of your daughter, sister, or cousin.

Lydia turned around just before I reached them and I could see tears stained on her cheeks already. I walked over to her and gave her a slight smile and rubbed her back a few quick times.

"Shall we get started, Lydia, or do you want a few more minutes?" Lydia picked up her hand to wipe it across her nose and sniffled in before she replied. I saw her kick the ground and thought maybe she was changing her mind, but then she began to speak.

"No, let's begin so we can get this over with."

"Okay." I gently touched her arm and then looked up to

find Seth sitting in the hoe, awaiting my permission to start digging. I nodded toward him and he began to walk the machine to the gravesite to start moving the headstone and slab and begin digging. Conner stood back respectfully and I shot a nod and glance toward him for a quick greeting. He gave a quick nod back in response and then crossed his hands in front of himself and stood quietly, waiting.

"Lydia, why don't we move back just a little bit so Seth has room to lay Cristina's slab and headstone, then we won't be in the way of the moving bucket either." She nodded and then began to turn toward me, so I began to walk more toward Conner. We all took our stands side by side and watched as Seth started to work away at unburying her dead daughter's remains.

Chapter Eleven

The hum from the hoe swinging effortlessly through the air along with the soft sounding thud as the dirt started to pile on itself beside the grave was something soothing to me. Maybe it was because of how many times I've listened to it over the years or maybe it was something that just soothed my soul.

I looked over to see how Lydia was doing and the look on her face was the complete opposite to my soothing feeling. I could distinguish a few looks down to uneasy, disturbed and disgusted. I'm sure there was more but I had only known this woman maybe three hours and those were the most obvious ones that I could pinpoint.

"Are you doing okay, Lydia?" I gently squeezed her shoulder again and felt her lean into my touch.

"Yes, I'm okay." She continued to gently sniffle back tears. She wore dark sunglasses now to cover her eyes but you could still see the trails that the tears left on her cheeks while they ran and fell to the ground.

Seth was making good time and soon the light tap from the hoe bucket colliding with the cement barrier, would clink. We always buried the caskets within a cement tomb. This was to keep anything and everything out of it and the caskets and bodies to remain peacefully rested without being disrupted. The only way to move the slab of course was with a hoe and a chain. The scrape of steel and cement was louder than normal and Seth hauled the bucket out of the hole and set it down on the ground.

He jumped out with a few chains to attach to the bucket before he would lower it in and rest it on the slab to finish hooking it up.

You could hear the steel clinking against itself and before I could even take a few deep breaths, he was already hooked up and back in the hoe lowering the bucket down into the ground. He soon jumped back out and unhooked a small collapsible ladder and lowered it into the hole. Seth was trained to do all of this himself. We never wanted to make a huge commotion or stir up more emotions on causing a parade out of something, when it was possible for one sole body to do it themselves.

"Okay, so once he's done attaching the chains to the top of the slab, he will retreat back out of the hole and get back in before slowly lifting the top cement slab out and placing it on the ground. This will give us a view of the casket and then he will follow sort of the same suit as hooking up the cement slab but we will not use chains on the casket. Instead there are two heavy straps that will wrap around and almost cradle it. This way we can bring it out carefully without any damages done to the casket. Once it is out, we will break the seal and open the lid. I do need to prepare you for the smell because it is one like no other. So, if you need to stop at any time, please let us know and we can wait. Once the casket is opened, we will run a hose from the casket down into the tank that is buried in the ground along the bush line. This will empty all the liquids away so we can look at what's inside of the casket. In this case, your broach. If you're unable or don't want to look into the casket, we can empty all the items and bring them over to you for you to view. Please don't worry about anything being sucked down into the tank; there is a metal wire mesh on the end of the hose that will be sucking with little tiny pinholes the size of pen ballpoints, so nothing can enter into it other than liquids. If you're ready when Seth comes out, I will let him know to carry onward with everything until its open, unless, of course, you need to stop."

Lydia looked white as a ghost. I totally understood it, everything I had just said is something nobody should ever have to hear in their lifetime, let alone experience and live it. She didn't say a word just slowly started nodding her head. I looked over toward Conner who still stood quietly with his hands crossed.

I heard Seth's feet hit the ladder and knew he would be popping out of the hole in a few short seconds. When he reached the top, he pulled the ladder out and laid it down on the ground beside the hole. This was to avoid the cement knocking it down or getting anything snagged on one another. He looked at me before continuing on back into the cab of the hoe. I nodded toward him and he gave me a returning nod before turning back around and heading back to the hoe to climb inside.

I heard the machine rev higher and saw the chains tighten and I knew the slab was on its way to being lifted off of the tomb that held Cristina Waytes casket. It didn't take longer than five minutes and you could see the dirt stained top poke out of the hole. I heard Lydia take a big deep inhale in and let out a sharp exhale. Seth laid the slab down on the ground and jumped out to unhook the chains and slab. He quickly worked away and then jumped back into the hoe to lower the boom back down the hole. His feet hit the ground and he was down the ladder and into the hole, hooking up the casket so it could be brought up by the slings. You could hear him fumbling around but it was quiet compared to the running machine that stood nearby. He appeared again within five minutes and followed the same routine. The hoe revved up and the boom started rising out of the six-foot hole.

I was watching Seth maneuver everything so intently, it took me a second to realize the pressure that I felt on my hand was from Lydia grabbing onto my hand. I looked over toward her and she was chewing on her bottom lip while nervously shifting her weight between her feet. A few more moments and she would see her daughter's casket hanging in midair.

This was the last moment of fantasy. All this was about to become true with a harsh slap of reality. Shit was literally about to smack her in the face and hit the fan. I gave her hand a quick squeeze and then the pearl white casket rose out of the hole in the ground.

Chapter Twelve

Cristina Waytes' remains now hung about four feet above the ground in a pristine pearl white casket. I must admit, these hefty bitches that people paid thousands for, well, they actually did pay for themselves. It looked as though maybe it was dirty from ground water and dirt, but there was no damage and no color fade and this thing had been in the ground for years.

Lydia and I still had our hands clenched when Seth started to lower the casket to the ground. I decided to let Lydia know that this was the time that we would need to head over and crack open the lid to start emptying the liquids and looking for their family broach.

"So, when the casket is fully sitting on the ground, we will go over and stand beside it. Seth will break the seal, open the lid, and then we will begin to put the hose into the casket to start the draining process. Again, this is where things start to get very hard, as the smells that will come from the casket will be one of no other." I looked over to see her tear stained pale face and then back toward Seth and the casket that was now resting on the ground. Seth idled down the hoe and then it was completely shut off, leaving nothing but the blissful noise of birds chirping and the leaves slightly rustling to the breeze that blew threw them every now and then.

"If you're ready, we can start making our way over." Lydia tightened her grip on my hand and then nodded her head. We started to take the walk that would scar Lydia for the rest of her life. Haunt her until her days became nothing. This wasn't something that you ever got use to or became okay with, it was something that would destroy you slightly and take a little piece of you and keep it always.

I didn't have to look over to instruct Conner of anything, he knew his job and his duties. He was run through them until it all became the lyrics to a well-known song. He would remain where he was unless something went wrong but he was never to disturb what little peace was left when opening a casket that was just pulled from the ground.

It didn't take us long to reach our destination. I could feel the energy shift between all of us and it became wary and tense, all which was normal to me at this point in my life and career. Seth bent down with a crow bar and started to slither it into the crack between the lid and the body of the casket. You could hear creaking as he gently pushed and pulled up and down before the loud bang came through, when the seal finally let go. Lydia jumped at the noise but Seth and I remained the same. He stepped back to lay the crowbar down and out of the way before he would gently lift the casket lid.

I could see liquid slowly spilling over the edges and running down the sides but something was wrong and different. There was something missing here. I could feel the puzzled look come across my face and glanced up toward Seth to see him making the same face.

There was no smell. The decaying death smell that you never forgot but always wanted to rid yourself of, it wasn't here. This casket was cracked open, there was liquid running down the sides, and if there were a smell, it would've hit you in the face like a slab of bricks and burnt your nose hairs. What in the actual fuck?! I felt my heart beat thump a little harder and tried to calm myself down before making too many assumptions or flying into complete panic mode. I was the professional one here; I couldn't start the freak out train with a distraught mother standing beside me.

Seth came back over and slowly started lifting the lid, revealing the inside contents of the casket. My stomach turned; there was nothing but murky water. When you have muscles and cells, all sink and decay off of your bones, there's silt and slimy liquid that floats alongside, inside, and on top of the ground water, it's not just water. Something was seriously wrong here. Seth turned to me with a panicked look and I nodded quickly to make sure he knew that I felt the same but not to alert Lydia just yet. All she knew was that this was all normal other than the smell that I had just drilled into her head, literally being omitted from this whole situation. I cleared my throat and pulled down my sunglasses from off of my head and placed them on my eyes.

"Seth, can you please gather the hose and get it in there to drain?" He looked like he was scared of what the hell was in there and as though he may get bit from the unknown water sitting in the casket.

I heard the pump start and then saw him carrying the hose over before plopping it into the casket. This only ever took usually two minutes before you could start to see items or bones. This meant that it wouldn't take long to show us what was going on.

I let go of Lydia's hands and grabbed my own. I could feel they were becoming clammy the more nervous that I became. The two minutes were up and the scene was becoming more and more sickening to me. Seth stepped away and I heard the pump shut off.

"What's going on? You still have liquids in the casket; don't you have to drain it all?" Lydia's question caught the attention of Conner which made him leave his post and start heading in our direction. Before I could answer, Seth walked back over and stopped beside me, while peering into the casket. Conner arrived shortly after and even he knew that something was different and not right. I soon could tell Lydia now knew something was up and the shift in her uncomfortableness to flustered became increasingly aware to everyone.

"Does this mean what I think it means, Laylin?" Seth asked his question as calmly as he could. The lump in my throat was almost choking me, man I wish I had one of our water bottles to help make the lump more bearable.

"It does, yes." My response was barely finished when Lydia became unhinged.

"What the fuck is going on with you people!? What is happening right now!? I demand you to tell me now!"

I couldn't be upset with her, but I honestly couldn't even fathom in my own brain what the fuck was happening and taking place here. I slowed my breathing and exhaled through my mouth slowly before replying so I could say it as carefully and professional as I could.

"Lydia, there is no smell, there is no variances between ground water or bodily fluids, skin, muscles, or anything other than murky ground water. We have drained the casket halfway and there is no evidence of anything arising or showing up." Lydia's scream caught me off guard.

"What the fuck does that mean!? That doesn't mean anything to me! What are you even talking about!? What are you saying!?"

I looked at Seth, then Conner, and then grabbed my own

hands again before placing them back in front of me.

"Lydia, that means that there is no body in your daughter's casket. By the looks of how everything is sitting in here, there never even was a body placed in this casket."

Chapter Thirteen

The wailing cries of a mother who had just lost her baby arose from Lydia as she stay kneeling on the ground with her head in her hands, in a pile of tears. I've heard it time and time again and it is one of the most heart wrenching sounds you could ever come across.

It had become all fresh again with a disturbingly new detail. Her teenage daughter's body hadn't even been left in the casket, something had gone on to have messed with a corpse after they literally showed the family that she had been laid to rest six feet under the ground and buried in a pile of dirt. It was even recorded and marked down in legal paperwork claiming the body had been buried and placed to remain in this plot until the end of all days.

What the fuck happened!? It was in a sealed cement vault, that means that no way in hell could someone just dig her up with a shovel and help themselves. It was professionally sealed as well, this meant that it couldn't just open easily. For god's sake, we had to open an exhumed casket with a damn crowbar!

"I'll be right back, Seth." He nodded and I started to head back toward the Tahoe. I needed that damn water now to wash down the bile that was threating to come up. In all my years and this was now sickening to me too.

Conner had already dispatched, explaining the situation and we were instructed by the chief not to move or touch anything else, as this was now deemed an ongoing crime scene investigation. Not even sure what we would do or touch, we had never come across such a uniquely sick situation ourselves either. There were already numerous cop cars on route and I'm sure the news was bound to try and cross the road block barricades within an hour or two, after watching the scene of cop cars coming up and toward the cemetery.

I reached the driver's side door and unlocked it and hopped in. The wailing from Lydia stopped with the door closure and the quiet stillness started to comfort me. I reached down into my center console and grabbed a fresh bottle of water and cracked it open before I began to have big gulps. I finished after five gulps and wiped my mouth with the back of my hand. I let a sigh leave my mouth as I leaned my head back against the headrest. I peered down and out the right side of the windshield, to see Conner trying to comfort Lydia and Seth now sitting on the hoe's track with his hand on his head. We all felt it. This was insanely screwed up and life was just deeming to keep creating such savage and harsh circumstances and turns for Lydia Waytes.

After a few moments of silence, I picked up my phone to dial the funeral homes number. It was only noon and it already felt like it had been an all-day occurrence. Probably from the amount of emotions that just showed up with one crack of a casket.

"Guardian Angels Funeral Home, this is Ayda, how may I help you?" Ayda's voice always seemed to help a situation; it just had that soothing something that people always seemed to search for.

"Hey, it's Laylin. Something pretty major has happened down here at the cemetery for today's exhumation, so Seth and I will probably be here for most of the day and maybe even partly after it. Is there any new cases or pickups or emergencies?" Before I totally clued into what I was doing, I noticed my reflection in the rearview mirror to show that I was actually rubbing my forehead back and forth. Self-soothing techniques now, nice. Wasn't even my family or daughter and it was stressing me out.

"No, ma'am. Nothing has been booked in or announced and nothing until next week for a family meeting/viewing and everything here seems pretty much done already today. So, just a slow maintain clean day." Ayda sounded joyful but without the rubbing it in your face tones. Man, on some days I sure loved this woman. She kept everything always in check and running smoothly and it helped me immensely, especially when days turned into one like todays.

"Okay, perfect. Are you able to look into funeral home records for me and pull up Cristina Waytes' file and record? She's the only one in there and was buried in 2004 for reference. Once you find it, can you send me over the whole case file? The cause of death, when her body was released from hospital and picked up for the funeral home, how the cleanup and preservation of her body went, the viewing. Literally every single thing in that case record, please send it to my email so I can have it on my phone." I grabbed the water bottle to have another quick sip of water before listening to Ayda's reply.

"Yes, I can do that for you right away. Is everything okay?" I heard her voice kind of waiver. This was a new one but I guess so was me asking for every explicit detail on a file of a deceased body for an exhumation.

"No, it is certainly not okay, but I can't talk right now so will catch you up probably tomorrow when I see you at work. I doubt we will be back at any reasonable time today." I sighed again as I hit the last of my words. We shared a few more words and I thanked her before hanging up and putting my phone on my lap. I could hear the faint hum of sirens and knew the clan would be arriving up here in a few short minutes.

I sat forward and grabbed another couple water bottles to haul back over to everyone in case anyone wanted a drink. This was about to be a long-drawn affair and we'd already been here for a few hours. Along with this sickening turn of events, someone may appreciate a drink of water. I hopped back out of the Tahoe and just as I closed my door, I saw the first police car enter into the parking lot. It didn't take long for seven more cars and a few black SUVs to follow suit. I locked the Tahoe and started heading back toward the gravesite.

I let a few long slow breaths out as I took my first few steps. "Here we go."

Chapter Fourteen

It didn't take me long to get back over beside Seth, Conner, and Lydia. The parking lot was now littered with police cars and the few dark SUVs that were associated with the crime scene investigators. I handed one bottle of water to Seth and another to Conner. Lydia was still in a heap of herself upon the ground and didn't even move or navigate her head to look anywhere but the ground. This woman was completely broken and destroyed inside and out. Her whole world had now been totally ripped apart shred by shred, twice in one lifetime. I honestly didn't know what else this woman could take. I knew that she wouldn't leave, not until she got more answers but I didn't think she'd be able to listen to how they would be talking about her deceased daughter and the hundreds of different possibilities of what went on and could have happened with her body. Now that this had turned from a routine exhumation to a full-on crime scene, she was able to go home. No one would make her stand by and watch, most of the time they would actually encourage family members to go home so they wouldn't have to be a part of something so technical and heartless.

 Investigations were done to the best interest of every party involved, but the words that were used and associated with such savage and gruesome tasks; they were labelled less than anywhere near sensitive or caring.

 I stood by Seth as we watched nine men follow each other into the cemetery and over to the gravesite. Three of the men were dressed in their casual business attire but in all black, which screamed investigator. One held a camera case, another a leather briefcase and another had a lit cigarette in between his fingers. It wouldn't be long and there would be yellow caution tape all around this site and nothing would be moving in or leaving out. Everything was about to become locked down, shut in and temporarily owned by the investigation crew and police officers.

"Ma'am, I'm Chief Eric Mulch, you must be Lydia?" Eric Mulch bent down to place his hands on Lydia's arm and back. She nodded her head through her sobbing and Eric picked up his head to look around at us. Conner had already informed all of them as to what led up to our discovery and everything that was already done and had gone on. We had nothing more to say except wait to be talked to, called on or instructed to help answer any more questions they would have or come up with.

"Lydia, can I help you stand up? We have some supplies to help make you more comfortable and we'd like to take you over to one of the trucks to sit for a while, if that would be all right?" Lydia let out another soft head bob and Eric looked back at two of his guys who stood behind him. They walked over and helped pick Lydia up and out of the dirt like she had been severely injured or beaten and needed assistance to move. The string of snot and tears left a fresh trail as two cops held her arms and back as she slowly drug her feet across the ground, while keeping her head hanging low so you couldn't see her face.

What an absolute stupid messed up sickening day! This was beyond screwed up and whoever did this to people deserved to be put into the ground and never allowed to come back up.

"Laylin Brown?" Eric walked over with his hand outstretched toward me. I took it gracefully and gave it a quick shake before pulling my hand back into my body and crossing my arms.

"Yes."

"Laylin, can you explain to me a little more of your findings? Conner gave us the basic run down of the operation and how everything went down, but I just want to record you, being funeral owner and the one who is proceeding with the exhumation today of Cristina Waytes." The two men that were in black were already starting to unpack their cases and one had already gotten his camera almost ready to start shooting and taking pictures.

"I can, yes. Umm, we started the exhumation like any other. We locate the correct plot number and get the hoe to start digging after we have removed any stone or slab that may be lying on top or in front. Once dug, we remove the top cement slab that encases the casket and then we lay that on the ground beside the hole and dirt that was pulled from the hole. Then we hook up the casket with a sling to remove it from the ground below and bring it to ground level to open it. We then use a pry bar to break and crack the seal, which allows us to open the casket lid." The click and flash of the camera broke my attention and I turned to see the operator of it standing over the casket snapping picture after picture.

"Please continue." Eric's voice brought me back over and I felt embarrassed that I lost track of what I was saying.

"Yes, my apologies. Once the casket is opened, the smell usually is the first thing to be prominent and very in your face even before the casket lid is opened to reveal what's left inside. Normally by the time exhumations are done, there is still some sort of body tissue left but severe decomposition. In this case, Cristina Waytes was buried seventeen years ago, so there was to be nothing found but body fluids, ground water, bones and the items that were laid to rest with her the day of her funeral procession. Today, we were on the look for a family broach that had been put into the casket with Cristina Waytes. Her mother, Lydia, was the one who wanted the exhumation to happen and was here to witness and see the broach for herself. When we opened the casket, the first tell-tale sign that something was wrong was that there was no smell." Eric cleared his throat before announcing his question.

"But that could've just meant it dissipated with being underground for all those years though, couldn't it?"

"No. The body was incased within a tiny box. Yes, ground water is able to seep into it but the full decomposition of the body and the fluids left floating among the water will always carry the decaying death smell. Always. There are no variations to smells; it always is that of death and decaying bodies." I watched Eric's face turn a slight tinge of green before he swallowed and nodded his head to continue me on with my statement.

"Once we noticed the smell wasn't present, we cracked the casket carefully and opened the lid. Once the lid was opened was when we definitely knew that something was seriously wrong with the situation. The water was indeed cloudy and dirty like ground water, but there was no residue of body fluids or decomposition. There was no slime or silt floating on top or among the water. We decided to drain half the casket to reveal any bones that would start to come to the surface with the water level decreasing and being drained out. Our hose that we have has metal wire mesh on the end with tiny pen point sized holes halfway. We could see there were no bones, no items or any sign that a body had even been buried inside of the casket. There was no clothing traces, no hair particles, the casket pillow did not even have any staining or permanent imprinting of a head solidly laying until completely decomposing into just a skull. Nothing was and nothing is in that casket." I finished my statement and shoved my glasses back on top of my head so I could make the day a little brighter. Anything to try and make this day not seem so dark. I didn't know exactly what to do; the need to soothe myself repeatedly was becoming stronger and stronger.

"Okay, thank you, Laylin. I just have to ask for your worker Seth's statement and then we can go into the next steps moving forward for us here today and then the next steps after today."

I nodded toward him and continued to watch the police officers walk around taking notes, pictures, and hanging caution tape. So much for the smooth, fast running exhumation that I had highly hoped and was assuming was going to happen and take place. Maybe next time, I'd just keep my mouth shut before I caused such a sickening jinx.

Chapter Fifteen

Seth's statement to the chief of police, Eric Mulch, didn't take that much longer than the one that I gave to him. Of course, it enlisted a few more details as he was the one operating the hoe and seeing firsthand the cement slab, the condition of the casket, and everything in between, far, and near. He was the first person to uncover everything and we were the first to notice that this casket was just an empty box full of nothing but water. Expensive resting place for ground water, which was initially meant to fully sustain and house Cristina Waytes' body until it lay peacefully inside as nothing more than bones and nasty liquid.

"Thanks, Seth." Eric turned and headed back over to where his guys were standing and working away at going over everything that was around from the top blades of grass to the density of the dirt down in the hole. Seth walked back over to the hoe track and we both sat down beside each other, each of us not saying a word. I picked my head up and looked across the cemetery to see Lydia looking distant and disassociated with a blanket held around her and the red and blue flashing lights illuminating her with every strobe that went around.

My heart ached for her. What a place to be, what a thing to have taken place and happened. Coming to terms with seeing your deceased daughter as bones and liquid, to your world being shattered knowing that her body didn't even get to lay to rest the day she was buried. It was like the day that never finished. There was no solidarity to it, it had been started and set up to finish the end of a mourning week of learning your daughter was never coming home, to being ripped open into a haunting dream of closure taken away in the blink of a second. It was beyond the lines of sadistic. The curve between insanity and keeping your shit together, the one pure piece of knowing that could tear your very existence apart and keep your mind on a wild chase of its own tail indefinitely. Yet, here we were, watching Lydia live it all. My heart broke for her was the biggest understatement of the year and I wish I could just fathom the words to give it the justification that it deserved.

Seth patted the top of my hand and it snapped me out of my distant stare toward Lydia sitting in the parking lot among a few police officers. I took a deep breath and let out a sigh.

"This is only the beginning you know?" Seth was a smart kid, so the statement leaving his mouth didn't really surprise me.

"I know." I watched the officer's work carefully and meticulously around the grave. They took finger prints off the casket and anything that could've been touched and left a trace. Seth's name and fingerprints were automatically being deemed innocent and off the case or so we were told right before they started sweeping for them. Seth had always worn gloves before starting work so I would be surprised if there were even any of his prints left on anything.

Eric turned his head and looked at Seth and me while he was still speaking with one of his fellow officers. They gave a quick nod and looked back at one another before he started to head back toward us.

"So, we will stay here and do our rounds of everything and continue to go over it with all of our tools, take pictures, basically our whole routine."

"Okay." My voice almost sounded squeaky and I was taken aback a little bit. The professionalism was dwindling and the anxiety exhaustion was starting to overtake I see. Eric looked at the ground before he said anything else and held some hesitation on his face which made my stomach turn.

"Is there something wrong, Chief?" My question made him raise his head and look directly at me while releasing his own long sigh.

"We have looked through the case file on Cristina Waytes, it looks like the old funeral home owner and mortician has passed away, so questioning him will be a little difficult. We are trying to track down the embalmer and funeral hand that day but haven't had any success up to this point. It seems as though everyone who ever worked in the funeral business from around here, once retired, moved as far away as they possibly could and severed as many ties possible, especially the ones that bound them to here. Some say coincidence, but in the scenario we are facing right now, I would say likely not. Because of the circumstances with the deceased mortician that's signature and name is on everything and the workers we can't find, we will need to dive deeper and continue an ongoing investigation. What this means for you and your funeral home, is we need full cooperation." Eric stopped talking and looked at me as though I would decline or interject his last statement. There was nothing I wanted more than the justice for Lydia and Cristina Waytes, there was absolutely zero hesitancy on my end.

"Yes, that's all completely understandable and okay with me. Whatever you need from me, the funeral home or any workers, you just let me know." Eric nodded and then cleared his throat. Every notion he included as he got deeper within his conversation, made me feel sicker and sicker with each passing moment.

"Laylin, we are going to need to perform eight more exhumations in this cemetery. The timelines from when they were buried will differ drastically, ranging back from times like Cristina's burial, all the way up until last Sunday's burial." I felt a dry lump stop in the middle of my throat and it felt as though it would gag me. He must've noticed the look of horror on my face because he decided to continue on before I could say anything.

"I understand how difficult this will be not only for you but for this town, the families and the families that will have to wait until all the exhumations are finished before any more funeral proceedings will be able to take place. This cemetery is now shut down for investigations until we have concluded all eight exhumations and have finished checking over every burial and body that we choose that lay rest here in these plots. I also understand that some families will want to decline but this being an ongoing investigation and police matter; they will simply have to comply if it is indeed, their deceased family member that is being chosen for one of the eight to be pulled from the ground. I will need your help in calling the families and letting them know. No families will be present while doing the exhumations; we need the cemetery as clear as it possibly can be. You and Seth will be the only ones from the funeral home permitted to be here during the process. We are shutting every funeral proceeding and this cemetery down for one week. We will not exceed the one week and everything will be back to how it needs to be by the end of that week. We will be starting immediately, tomorrow to be exact. You will also need to make an announcement to let people know that the funeral home will not be participating or putting on any services from tomorrow until the week is through. We will be offering compensation for the families of the deceased that we are pulling back up and disturbing. This will be a small compensation for the disturbance of not only their family members laid to rest but for the disturbance that they will have with the uncomfortable knowledge of it all. Each family will receive compensation in the amount of five thousand dollars from the town and it will be delivered in check form and given promptly. I need to look over the list of case files to decide which bodies will be exhumed. Is there a time today when we can go over the list that works for you? And do either of you have any questions?" Eric looked back and forth at Seth and me while we both sat silently in a feeling of drowning. I could only presume Seth was feeling the exact same way as me. This was about to become the worst week that created the worst year in both of our lives. Having to be a part of such a chain of exhumations for an investigation and what if it wasn't normal like Cristina's? What if more bodies had been robbed from their graves?

"We can leave now if you're able to and can go look at the case files and print off the ones you are wanting to investigate and exhume. We can go in my work truck or you can follow me to the funeral home in your own vehicle, whatever is easier and works best."

"Now works fine. I will grab my stuff and ride with you." I nodded toward him and turned to look at Seth who sat looking super pale and uncomfortable.

"Do you want me to get you anything to eat on our way back or do you need anything? I can pick it up for you since it seems as we may be here for a while still." Seth slowly nodded his head and I thought I was going to have to ask him the same question again but then he slowly and quietly began to speak.

"Please bring me some food; everything else is in the truck so that's fine. Just any kind of food and a protein drink, please." I grabbed Seth's shoulder and gave it a quick squeeze before getting up off the track hoe and looking back at Eric.

"You ready?" Eric nodded and we both started to make our way silently across the cemetery and toward the parking lot. He veered to the left to go grab his things from his car and I hopped into the Tahoe and started it while I waited for him. I laid my head back against my headrest and pulled my sunglasses back down over my eyes. I started to take some deep breaths to help keep my composure. I felt like I wanted to cry but also like I could get sick.

Chapter Sixteen

The ride to the funeral home was quiet. Eric sat quietly in the passenger seat occasionally checking his phone every time it buzzed and went off. For some reason, I felt like I was on trial. It was even to the point of feeling like I was sixteen again and taking my driver's test with how he would sometimes glance over my way and check out the speedometer. Or maybe he wasn't, and it was all in my head. This day's level of stress went from a small percentage to a full-blown hurling ball of freak out, so yeah could be my mind just extra panicking and freaking out.

"You can relax, Laylin, I'm not here to observe you or take notes of your driving skills. This is simply a work matter and not an audit of you." Eric's face never broke from the seriousness stillness it held but there was a warmth gesture to his tone.

"It's that obvious, huh?" A small smirk sat on my lips and I glanced over my right shoulder quickly to look at him. The corners of his mouth lifted into a small smile.

"I've been doing this job for a long time, so it becomes quite obvious, yes. Even hard for people to act normal and not be nervous when I'm not on duty and just being my regular self, not in cop mode."

"Hard to never not be noticed then." The air became a little less tense, as I finished my last word and I felt my shoulders relax a little bit and drop back down to their normal position.

Even if he did seem nerve wracking and scary, he did have a genuine character and a sweet soul. Seemed like someone you could just talk to for hours if you needed to. Even if you were guilty, it seemed as if he would still look at you as though you were a human being, which was very rare and hard to find in today's world.

My turn signal blinked off as I turned into the parking lot of the funeral home. It didn't take us long to unbuckle our seatbelts and hop out, once I had the Tahoe in park and the ignition turned off.

"These doors always remain locked twenty-four seven?" Now here were the cop investigation questions arising.

"Yes. We never leave them unlocked. There are very few circumstances when waiting for family members that the doors may be left unlocked but rarely ever are. We have the unlock switch at the front desk by my receptionist Ayda and when she sees clients or anyone needing in, she unlocks the doors and they come on in. Otherwise, the staff all have their own door fob that you hold in front of the strip and it unlocks the door for you momentarily." Eric nodded and I pulled the door open and held it for him. I followed him inside and we headed into the reception area.

The look on Ayda's face was one of nervousness and confusion. There was never a cop to accompany me to my funeral home during an exhumation, so there were a lot of unanswered questions floating among us. I nodded toward her and she smiled back toward Eric and I. Eric returned the favor with a small nod toward Ayda.

"It's this way, Eric." I continued on walking toward my office as he slowed down just before he got to the front desk. I heard his footsteps pick up again and then we reached my doorway. I walked through the doorway and grabbed one of the guest chairs to haul around and place beside my office chair. If we were going to be scrolling through thousands of casefiles to choose from, it would be a lot more comfortable and easy with us both sitting side by side and on the same level.

"Please, have a seat and I'll get logged in and everything pulled up to start looking through everything." Eric removed his jacket and hung it on the back of the chair and I stepped in between to sit in my office chair. He sat down about the same time as my butt hit the chair and I slid back to hit the back of my seat.

"Once you're in, am I able to take over scrolling so I can control everything rather than trying to direct you to click or go back? It would just speed up this process and get us back out to the cemetery sooner than later." I nodded in agreement and started to get everything logged in and set up so that I could push my chair back and out of the way for him to start his search. Anything to help speed up this process to get us back out there to hopefully help figure all this crap out.

I clicked my last button and the case files all loaded alphabetically and I pushed my chair back. Eric grabbed his chair and shuffled it over so he could sit directly in front of the computer. I turned back and grabbed a protein shake from my fridge and cracked it open. Man, I loved myself for always buying these and keeping them stashed in here. For reasons exactly like today being I forgot how hungry I was until I realized I drank over half of it with my first crack of opening it.

I sat quietly looking around my office and just enjoying the moments of not needing to do anything. Eric was engulfed in my computer screen and I wasn't saying anything to distract him. I was good with leaving him be to get everything he needed without me posing any distractions to him. My printer went off a few times and spit out sheets of paper here and there, I lost count of how many times he had hit print. It had to have been close to eight casefiles because there was already a good amount of papers sitting on my desk in front of the printer where they had come out.

"Okay, that's the last one, you can log out and I will gather them all up and we can head back out." Eric's sudden voice made me jump as I was lost in thought staring at the cracked paint in the corner of my office.

"Okay, sounds good." Eric stood up and moved away from the computer so I could finish the process of logging off and shutting down my computer. He grabbed the papers and tidied them before placing them down on the desk and grabbing his jacket. I hit the log out button and reached down to shut off my computer monitor screen. Who knew how long Seth and I would be at the cemetery for today, may as well turn everything off so we could both just head home once we were cleared and able to leave. I stepped back and grabbed another protein shake for Seth and grabbed the rest of my things and nodded toward Eric. I appreciated the nodding, it was a silent communication that we both seemed to each understand and it saved energy from speaking when we really didn't have to. He reached down and grabbed the stack of paperwork on the desk and we began heading toward the front door. One quick stop to grab food for Seth and I, then we'd be back to the panic-stricken gravesite. This was the first day in a long time where I was actually awaiting and wanting this day to end and be able to go home. This week was going to be one of the longest of my life.

Chapter Seventeen

As we neared the ending of the road to the cemetery, you could see multiple news vehicles, along with just snoopy people parked on the side of the road on this side of the police barricade. They knew they could not pass the barricade without facing a fine and now that it was an active crime scene, actual charges incurred onto them. This usually meant people didn't even chance stepping one foot over the police barricades and boundaries.

"And here are the producers of our reality crime scene show." Eric let out a sigh as he hit the end of his sentence. I wasn't sure if he was trying to make a joke out of the situation but if he was, I surely didn't find it funny. All the traffic and commotion was starting to make me feel even more uncomfortable and panicky.

I slowed the Tahoe down as I started driving between vehicles and people. Today was already stressful enough for me; I didn't need to add running someone over or knocking mirrors off of vehicles to my list. Harold moved the barricade for me so I wouldn't have to come to a complete stop and be bombarded at my driver's window and totally engrossed within people. I appreciated him so much more for this right now. I slowly passed through the barricades and lifted my fingers to wave at him as we carried forward.

"You know, Laylin, before we are done and you go home today, you will need to make a statement to reporters for the public. I understand the want to avoid situations like these but without the statement people will begin to panic, worry and then become furious and lashing out. We need to try and keep this situation as level headed as we possibly can. Especially with the circumstances of the situation, we don't need to rock the boat so harshly that we become completely capsized." All I could do was swallow in agreement. I knew Eric could wrap his head around what I was thinking and feeling and I was thankful he wasn't demanding of an answer to be given to him.

I pulled into the same parking spot that I parked in this morning at the cemetery and put the truck into park. We both got out of the Tahoe and started toward the gravesite. It looked as though we were on a movie set of a crime scene production. I hadn't ever been so close, up front and center with an active investigation and I must admit that it didn't make me feel all safe and secure. There were tons of police officers around and I felt anything but protected. This came startling to me as I literally played with dead bodies for a living and buried them into the ground or sent them off to be lit on fire. The weirdest things seemed to deeply disturb me and that in itself, made my inner core waiver.

Seth was now lying on the ground beside the hoe. There were a few officers beside him but no one seemed to have a problem with him and his waiting position. I walked up and crouched down near his head and touched his shoulder gently.

"There's a shake and some food in the truck for you. Why don't you go sit in there, eat and relax for a while? You could have a sleep if you needed, take some time and go sit in the truck, it'll help you. If we need something we can come and get you." Seth looked pale and almost terrified. I wanted to give him a hug but instead I just squeezed his shoulder before standing up and moving out of his way so he could get up and start toward the parking lot. I turned around to see Eric giving me a caring glance.

"Where is Lydia?" My question seemed to flip him back into full professional police chief mode.

"She was escorted home from one of my men. She insisted that she could stay, but she was not doing physically well anymore, so we made sure someone would be home waiting for her so they could watch her and she could rest." I nodded my head and reached my hand up to scratch the side of my head.

"So, what happens now, Eric?" I was starting to feel frustration creep in. It had nothing to do with Eric or his men but the complete feeling of this whole situation now being out of my control. Being a mortician and funeral home owner, I always had control and this was out of my comfort zone.

"Once we have finished investigating this specific grave of Cristina Waytes, we will start on the list of case files I have here and we will get you and Seth to help us exhume each grave. If nothing is found, we will lower them back in and rebury. If there is something wrong, like there is with Cristina's body, or the lack of any body, or plot they are in, then we will halt again and take everything we need from them and then decide if we are just refilling the hole or marking it off. We cannot leave six-foot holes open for animal or people's safety but we will have to determine if we need to seal it and take the caskets, bodies, or any other evidence with us or if we can simply put everything back in the ground and back to rest."

"Okay. So today will be more dedicated to Cristina Waytes and solely her case?" I placed my hands on my hips and took a wider more comfortable stance while I watched the once peaceful cemetery now looking like a room turned upside down with everyone scattered looking for the lost piece of a puzzle.

"That is correct and tomorrow we will start early with exhumations of others. We only have a short window, especially if there are others that have been tampered with or are completely missing like Cristina Waytes." Someone hollered and Eric turned his head to see he was being flagged over.

"Excuse me, Laylin." I turned away to study the casket and watch the investigators carefully going over each detail of it, along with the hole from where it came from. I didn't know what to do with myself. Maybe I should go lie down on the ground and just stare at the sky while I listened to people work away.

They probably wouldn't need me for the rest of the day and no one would be talking to me or informing me of any new discoveries. I was a major part in this but I was not anywhere on the totem pole to be able to have confidential police reports, until of course, they became public records that anyone could have access to.

I walked over to where I had found Seth lying down and sat down comfortably as I could. I leaned back on my hands and outstretched my legs in front of me. I peered over to see Seth still leaned back into the seat and it looked as though maybe he had been crying. This poor kid was only twenty-three and now would be traumatized from this for the rest of his life. It's one thing to become comfortable and understanding with death and what all parts take place when it happens. But to be put in the position to see a body be cheated out of being laid to rest, it was one of total violation. The world was sick enough, how the hell would you even feel peace now, knowing that your body would be robbed from your casket as soon as your family went home.

Chapter Eighteen

"Laylin?" I zoned back into reality to realize that Seth was now back standing beside me and calling my name. I picked my head up and propped my elbows on the ground to hold the top half of myself up to look at him. I decided halfway through my leaning back sitting pose that lying down was the most comfortable option. The care for my professionalism went out the window when I stopped wanting to watch people crawl around like bugs picking and prodding everything about Cristina's casket.

"Yeah? Sorry." Seth looked better; he must've calmed down enough and had some food and water. The color had returned to his face and he seemed more relaxed with everything.

"Did Eric talk to you about this week's plan?"

I nodded my head and pushed myself all the way up so I was back sitting upright. Seth walked the last few steps over and sat down beside me. I started to fidget with blades of grass before replying. I could feel the softness of the grass and then I would hit the little sticky tacky part and slide it under my nails. This always used to comfort me as a kid and I was relieved to see it still did the trick.

"Yes, I'm aware, he filled me in already. Are you okay? How do you feel about all of it?" I looked over at him to see he was now twirling grass between his fingertips too, while leaning forward on his crossed legs looking at the ground.

"It'll be fine, I just would like some time off afterwards. I know it'll be busy because we have to halt all proceedings for a week but I don't think I can just snap back into a normal work routine after this week. Especially if more turn up to be like Cristina Waytes situation." I reached out and squeezed Seth's hand before returning to the grass in front of me.

"That isn't a problem, Seth. I totally understand and wouldn't ask or expect anything different. If you weren't going to ask, I was going to suggest, so we are already on the same page with that. I will pay you for your time off as well. How about you start with a week off and by the last few days we catch up and see how you're feeling?" He nodded quietly and I saw a single tear run off his cheek. This day was starting to destroy me. Not only was it tangling up so many emotions but it was pulling pieces from people too.

"Laylin." The sudden sternness of my name being announced sucked me out of the sad pool I was starting to drown in with Seth. I looked up to see Eric standing off to the side looking at me.

"Yes, Eric?"

"It's time for you and me to head down to the barricades and give a statement to the news stations. We will go down there and do one press release and that will be it for today. You and Seth can pack up and head out after that's done. We will have the barricade down there 24/7 for the remainder of the investigation and officers taking shifts to man it. We are going to place the cement slab back on top of the tomb and bury Cristina's plot. The casket will be loaded and hauled back to the police station for further testing and investigation. So, if Seth is able to finish draining all the liquid out of it, that would be great, and then we can get everything loaded and packed up so we can all head back and get started early tomorrow. I'd like you two to be back here for eight a.m., please." I stood up before I turned back to look at Seth.

"Seth, can you finish draining and when I get back, I'll drive us back to the funeral home and we can head home."

Seth stood up and wiped his face before nodding and turning back toward the equipment to finish draining out the empty casket.

"Okay, let's go." Eric turned and we both started walking toward the parking lot.

"No names will be given out by you regarding the bodies that will be exhumed or Cristina's body that is missing. Keep it simple but straightforward. Remind people that they will be contacted if a loved one is going to be exhumed, but it will be done privately through the discretion of the funeral home. We will take my cruiser down and once you have finished your statement, we will come back up and you and Seth can head home for some much-needed rest before tomorrow."

I climbed into the passenger seat after Eric finished talking and his head disappeared into his driver's seat. I took a deep breath and steadied my nerves. I started to go over some things in my head so that I could almost have it remembered to a tee so nothing slipped up or forgot to mention something that needed to be said. I only had maybe two minutes before we got there, parked, and climbed out. The shortest two minutes of my life.

As we started to see the barricade, the swarm of people gathered quickly and like a flock of sheep running to exit their pen. My stomach twisted and I shifted nervously in my seat.

"It's okay, Laylin, it will be fine." I exhaled deeply toward my window before Eric came to a stop and put the car into park. I grabbed my door handle and stepped outside. I started to take the short walk to the front of the car and stopped on our side of the barricade. Microphones and cameras all started to show up and be pulled up and presented right in front of my face. I turned to make sure that Eric was standing close by. He was stopped just to the back left side of me and smiled slightly to let me know that I could begin. I cleared my throat and pushed some hair behind my ear.

"Hello, everyone, my name is Laylin Brown. I am the owner and a working mortician of the Guardian Angels Funeral Home here in town. Today, we were presented with unusual and conflicting circumstances for what was planned as a routine exhumation. Because of our findings, we have been launched into a full active ongoing crime scene investigation. This will remain an open case until matters are solved and laid to rest. A body has been deemed missing from a casket, that was recorded and filed as buried. It saddens us deeply of the trauma that is being inflicted not only on the family but to the idea of not even being safe with being laid to rest after departing from this world. Because of the details of this current situation, we are needing to make mandatory exhumations to check the status of a few random plots as well. We understand how difficult this can be and the plots that have been chosen, we will be reaching out to the families to discuss details further with them, under discretion from the funeral home. We are working very closely with the police and the investigators to find out the people responsible for these tragic and horrific events and we are doing our best to work diligently and quickly to get back to normal running operations. With that being said, the cemetery will be closed to the public for the days of the investigation and all funeral proceedings and processions will be placed on hold until everything is cleared up. The investigation will take approximately seven days to commence and finish. Again, with the duration of these seven days, we will not be conducting any funerals and no one will have access to the cemetery other than the police, myself, and one fellow funeral home worker. Thank you all for your time and patience while we work on putting everything back to rest peacefully and respectfully. Any more significant updates will be available to you by myself or the chief of police, Eric Mulch. Thank you all and have a good day."

The air felt heavy as I listened to all of the questions rise up from each and every one of the reporter's mouths, but I wasn't staying around to listen. I was already turned around and walking back to the passenger side of the car to climb in and head back up to the cemetery. I just hoped Eric followed suit and didn't expect me to stand there and answer questions.

I pulled my sunglasses down over my eyes and leaned my head back on the headrest and closed my eyes. If he was standing out there and there were awkward eyes staring at me, I didn't want to know. I heard the door open and felt the shimmy of the car before I heard it close again. Thank god, Eric was done and we were leaving back up to the cemetery and away from all this noise and bullshit.

"Well done, I couldn't have put it any better myself. I will send you home with all the numbers of the exhumations that will be taking place and I need you to place those calls tonight so we can continue moving forward tomorrow morning. I know it's been a lot and will continue to be a lot for the next week but once it's over, it'll be over." I took a few deep breaths in and exhaled slowly but calmly.

"I will place those calls tonight when I get home and keep record of whom I've talked to and what time." I kept myself in the same position and hadn't even opened my eyes yet. I felt the car start moving and decided to stay leaned back against the seat with my eyes closed.

"Thank you. You have no idea how much easier this becomes for us when we have a second party cooperating and helping us out so much. We appreciate both yours and Seth's efforts, so thank you."

I sat quietly listening to the rocks crunch under the tires as we drove over them. I was exhausted and I still had however more hours of work left to do when I got home. Eight families to talk to and explain the exhumation process and now an investigation process. I was going to need a glass of alcohol when I was done, followed by a hot shower and bed.

I felt the car slowing down and knew we were close to being parked back up in the cemetery parking lot. I took my last few tire motions to enjoy my few seconds of peace before getting out and continuing onward for the rest of the afternoon. I seemed so close to being done but so far from finishing this whole disturbing nightmare completely.

Chapter Nineteen

Eric pulled into a spot back in the cemetery parking lot and threw the car into park.

"So, I can take Seth and myself home now for the day and we will meet back here for eight tomorrow morning?" I grabbed my door handle to open the door and Eric and I both hopped out of the car. He stood looking over top of his roof at me before replying. I shut the door and stood awaiting his answer.

"Yes, you both can. Once the casket is drained, of course, and tonight you'll need to make those calls to those eight families." I stepped back and nodded. I turned to see Seth rolling up the hose and immediately knew that he was done draining the casket and would be able to head over to the Tahoe so we could head back to the funeral home.

"And do you have a number that I can reach you at incase the families are not willing or wanting to speak with me or have more in-depth questions that only you can answer?" My question propped him to start reaching into his pockets searching for something before he pulled out a card and reached it across his roof toward me. I took a few steps forward and leaned forward grabbing it from him.

"My personal cell is on there as well, after eight o'clock tonight that's the number you'll need to call if you need me. Please don't give my personal number to families but call and give me a heads up and I will call them back on my work phone."

"Okay, I will do that. Thanks, and I'll see you tomorrow." I stuffed the card into my hand that was currently holding my phone and grabbed my keys before turning back toward Seth in the cemetery standing over by the hoe. I started to wave my hand to flag him over and once he noticed me, he started walking without any hesitation. I started to walk to the Tahoe and hit unlock just before I grabbed the door handle. I climbed inside and started it up. The radio was still off and the quiet that came from the inside of this truck was so soothing to the loudness and commotion carrying on outside. Everything was muffled through the closed doors but the quiet still overtook the various muffled noises and talking that slipped through.

The passenger door opened and I looked to watch Seth climb into the passenger seat and shut the door behind him. He looked almost gray now and sat quietly looking out the window back into the graveyard.

"Are you okay, Seth?" I saw his hand go up and wipe another tear from his eye that was on the verge of running down his cheek.

"I'm okay. Just that final drain and then watching them come and take over everything to pack it up and load it to take with them to investigate. It's been a rough day, boss." I reached my hand over and rubbed the top of his back. There wasn't much I could say or do for him. I knew exactly how he felt and there was nothing that anyone could say or do to make me feel better. I felt violated and uncomfortable and it wasn't even my body that had been tampered with.

I grabbed the gear shift and put the Tahoe into reverse so we could get on our way and heading back toward the funeral home.

"Tomorrow, I'll need you to meet me at the funeral home

for seven thirty in the morning so that we can be back out here for eight o'clock in the morning to start the next exhumations. Hopefully, the rest will go smoothly and we can put all this to rest and get back on with our regular proceedings. Pack a big lunch because I have a feeling we will be here all day corresponding and helping with the investigation. Please keep the details to a minimum from friends and family so that you don't get into trouble with leaking information that is confidential to this investigation. We will get through this week, Seth, and then it will be done and over with. I know I can't make it all go away, but I am here going through it with you and we can lean on each other during it and after if we need to. Thank you for being here with me today. I know you didn't ask to be a part of something like this, but unfortunately it has turned into it and now we are here together to get through it. We can do this, I know we can." Seth turned his head to look at me and smiled before turning back around to continue to watch the trees go by as we carried onward toward the funeral home. This poor kid, I felt like I had completely destroyed him and it wasn't even my fault.

Chapter Twenty

I walked into my house and threw all my stuff down onto the counter. I walked over to my liquor fridge and pulled out a perfectly chilled bottle of red wine. I reached up and grabbed a wine glass and headed back over to my kitchen island to sit on my bar stool and crack open the new bottle.

I was normally a gin woman but the red wine was always a dear friend of mine. One that would slow the racing thoughts down and help ease my nerves. It was a good unnerving that was needed now from a long day of hardships and grey hair causers.

The silky pour and feeling the chill between my fingers as it filled the glass allowed me to let out a long-awaited sigh. I plopped the bottle down and picked up my glass to have a nice long swig. I felt the coolness pool into the bottom of my stomach and I felt a wave of tingles creep over my skin. I sat with the feeling for a few seconds before snapping back into reality.

Okay, eight families to call and explain that we were pulling up their dead family members to inspect them and make sure nothing wrong went on or to make sure that they were actually still in the ground. Oh, some days this job could take all its flaws and shove it so far up the world's ass.

I grabbed the stack of files and started to flip through them to see how recent and how far back they were going with the bodies that they were to begin digging tomorrow. I felt a gasp want to leave my soul when I saw that they were planning to exhume the body of a thirteen-year-old girl that was buried three weeks ago. She had been killed brutally when a drunk driver smashed into her family's car on their way home. I remember her clearly, she was such a beautiful girl and we were able to make her resting peaceful sleep look explicitly soothing to her survived family, that were faced with the unimaginable heartbreak of losing a child.

I wanted to die. Three weeks and a thirteen-year-old. This shit was so cruel. How was I supposed to take a freshly grieving family that lost their young daughter that had her whole life ahead of her and slam down on their table that she would indeed be brought back up from her resting place that she had just so recently been laid to rest in?

I picked up my glass and finished it off before placing it back down on the counter. I grabbed the bottle and filled it back up, almost to the brim. I pulled a hair tie out of my bag that still lay on the counter and tied my hair back. This was going to be a long night and I needed to get it done as quickly as I could so I could take my bottle of wine and comfort myself out of this hell hole of a nightmare that was seemingly stuck on repeat. I was talking a nice level of drunk to watch a happy movie and fall asleep with the distraction that tomorrow did not exist.

I reached down and grabbed my phone. I slid the thirteen-year-old girl's file off to the side and grabbed the other seven. I would start with the rest and make her family my last call, because I knew it would be the hardest one. Please let there be some almighty god that had protected these bodies, so these families wouldn't need to experience the second wave of pain that packs a punch harder than the first time because of the gaping hole of the existence of what ifs and the unknowing.

I looked down and started to type in the phone number from the first file. I took one more quick drink while I heard the first ring come across my phone. It didn't take long before someone answered. I sat forward and leaned my head into my hand on the counter for support. I took a quick exhale before I began my speech of disruption and disturbance to this family's life. The slight buzz of an empty stomach and red wine would hold my hand through it. I leaned in closer toward my phone that lay resting on the counter on speaker and awaiting my reply.

"Hello, this is Laylin Brown from Guardian Angels Funeral Home. I was hoping you had a moment so we could talk?"

Chapter Twenty-One

Seth and I rolled into the cemetery parking lot precisely at eight in the morning. He looked to have more life in him but the feeling and energy was that of the faintest. The glum mood seemed to be the new constant in our world since yesterday.

It looked as if more investigative vehicles had arrived and there was already people hurriedly working away and taping off the correct plots that we would be disturbing and digging up. The news crews had not dissipated at all and we had to do the regular slow crawl through the barricades, to make sure we didn't make breaking news for killing a reporter while heading to the cemetery. How ironic would that be?

Eric was heading over to the Tahoe and I shut it off and grabbed my stuff to meet him outside and on the hood.

"Laylin, I'm going to fire up the hoe and see where they want me start." I nodded back to Seth and brought my attention back to focus on Eric. I plopped the case files down on the warm hood of my Tahoe and lifted my sunglasses up to let them rest on my head. I shifted my weight to lean on my hip and against the vehicle. Eric followed suit and landed both elbows on the hood looking at me and the paperwork as I started to fan it out before explaining how last night's evening phone calls went.

"Ayda is doing up the paperwork for the families and writing the checks. Most preferred mail, so we decided to just mail all of them directly to the families. I was told the county would then be reimbursing the funeral home of all costs, once the checks were cashed and processed. Most families were in disbelief, disgust and shock. Some were angry but most of them accepting of the unfortunate circumstances. No one needed nor wanted to talk with you or hear any more information then they needed to, so I kept it as minimal as I could with explaining the full procedures. I also let them know that if something was to be off with their family members plot or body, you would be the one who would then be contacting them further." I swallowed and licked my lips before leaning my head into my hand.

I couldn't silence the amount of stillness that came through the phone from the family of the recently deceased and buried thirteen-year-old girl. The silence they portrayed was deafening to me and there was nothing in my mind of wisdom words that I could say to take away the re-break of their heartache. The situation in itself disturbed me, almost more than this whole situation that had led us to be doing all of this in the first place.

"Everything sounds good. We should be able to have most of the plots dug up and pried into today. We will have plastic covered tents to go over the holes and caskets until the investigation is over so that any weather does not alter or disturb the scene." I stood quietly with a minimal shift in my expression before grabbing my glasses to pull them back down over my eyes. I needed some sort of personal space and comfort ever since yesterday and it seemed to feel like it was so damn difficult to find. I was gathering up the last pieces of paperwork when Eric asked a question that stopped my fumbling fingers.

"Are you doing okay, Laylin?" I almost scoffed at the question but decided that would be mostly rude to someone who wasn't the reason for causing all this noise and commotion.

"Professionally or personally Eric?" He shifted his weight

and pulled his arms and body off the hood of my work truck, before widening his stance and crossing his arms.

"Both I guess."

"Well, personally, no, I am not. I had a whole bottle of wine lull me to sleep last night with a movie to take my racing brain away from this whole fucked up situation. Professionally speaking, we are all doing the very best that we can and we will be glad when everything and everyone can hopefully be laid to rest without any more exercises for extraction from the ground." Eric seemed to study me for a few moments before he sent a single nod my way to show he understood and where I was coming from. This was his every day. Exhumations of regular routine, well, that was part of my some days. This whole madness of a missing body and pulling dead people out of the ground like we were fishing for corpses, well that was a whole other side show and a half in itself.

Chapter Twenty-Two

I stood quietly listening to the chatter of people talking, the snaps of cameras, and the clicks of pens and the constant swinging of the hoe boom followed by soft thuds and clinking chains. There was not much for me to do but wait and see how all of this would unravel and what every casket would soon reveal about its contents and what it may be holding. Hopefully all of what it was supposed to be. I had never prayed so hard before in my life for a dead body to be where a dead body should be.

Seth was working meticulously away and I was damn proud of this young man continuing forward without hesitation and helping so diligently alongside the crime scene unit to help get this case worked on, dealt with and hopefully solved and closed.

The sound of the word "here" caught my attention and pulled me away from watching Seth place another cement slab down onto the ground beside a freshly dug six-foot hole. There were a few officers that quickly walked over to their coworker who was waving them over. Eric followed suit quickly and I felt my stomach twist into knots.

Another one? No fucking way was there another one! We were only on the third casket today and already someone was calling people over to take a look. Maybe there wasn't anything wrong; maybe they just wanted a second opinion. Yet these men were told to look for unusual particularly clear and clean ground water other than the small amounts of mud or silt from the ground, so no way in hell could the holler be a good sign. I took a quick swallow and decided to start heading over in that direction. Just as I was halfway there, I noticed Eric was turning around and searching for someone, at this point I could only assume that someone was me because indeed there was something wrong with another gravesite and body. As he saw that I was already on my way, he turned his attention back toward the casket.

As I neared the casket, I could tell this was the supposed resting place of a thirty-five-year-old woman buried two months ago. She had died after giving child birth; it was yet another tragic death not only to her family but to the fresh little baby that now endured life without the safety and comfort of its mother. I remembered this case quite well too, my worker Gregory worked on her and did an amazing and beautiful job. She looked ever so peaceful, and I remember her husband being so thankful and gracious for how wonderful his wife looked being laid to rest in her pretty midnight blue casket.

Seth was only pulling caskets and the members of the police force who were cracking the lids, were in charge of sucking out the caskets now. By the time I reached it, I could see the water level was already almost completely omitted from the casket and indeed there was something severely wrong with this casket and the body that lay within it.

It was in stages of final decomposition but you could still clearly see that both of her feet were cut clean off and no longer remaining inside her casket with her body. Her gorgeous head had also been taken and was no longer anywhere to be found. Now what lay inside this once-full, occupied casket was a footless, headless hunk of rotting flesh, muscles, and bone.

I felt the sweat start to pool in my hands and my stomach did another one eighty. How could I help these people find out what was happening to these bodies, when I couldn't even wrap my own brain around what the hell was going on here? There was obviously some very sick disturbed person that was exhuming these people and taking their whole bodies or limbs along with them, but who? How could it be my staff when the first body was from seventeen years ago? But then again, this woman was buried two months ago and my staff and I were the ones who were in charge of all of her after life care and it went off without a hiccup, or so I thought. Something was so severely messed up and I wanted to scream at the top of my lungs.

"You remember working on this body?" Eric's question startled me as I stared in horror at the now decapitated body in front of me.

"Yes, I do. She died in childbirth. It was a simple and quick recovery and embalming. My worker did the makeup and final touches and she looked so beautiful and peaceful and the service that followed was a success. We buried her in her plot and then we loaded our materials and headed home." Eric reached out and grabbed my shoulder. He must've noticed the tear forming in my eye before I did and tried to express some comfort. Obviously hiding behind my professionalism was no longer working and these continuous disturbing discoveries were starting to weigh on me personally and the whole crew around me was starting to notice it as well.

"Let's take a walk away from here, Laylin." I turned with Eric and reached up to wipe a tear before it started a stream down my face. I gave a quick sniffle and we started walking. I felt the air getting heavy and I knew the next conversation that was going to arise, was going to be one that I wasn't going to want to be a part of.

"So, now knowing we aren't just dealing with one body but two, let alone if others are deemed the same fate, this investigation will be going into full active mode. That means that everyone working for you and with you is going to be asked questions. I will need you to start watching your workers closely. This is especially true for the ones who retrieve the bodies and who embalm the bodies. We understand that you watch them be buried and everything is back to normal before leaving but with how clean those cuts were and equally decomposed, that body had its limbs severed shortly after it was supposedly locked into its vault and left to rest. We will need to wait to have the final results by the end of today, but moving forward you are now actively apart of this crime scene. You will be interviewed as well because it is protocol and everyone is needed to go through questioning. Yours will commence after the week is through. This is so you can carefully watch your staff, notice their clock in hours and when they leave. Look into the hours they worked around this case and any others that were done by your staff and funeral home. I want you to be able to tell me when they ate, scratched their head or brought in or dealt with a new intake. We need to figure this out and get it handled as soon as possible. The disturbance of deceased bodies is a disturbance beyond words and it won't sit well with anyone finding out their loved one was chopped up like they had been run through a butcher shop."

I was numb to his words. I couldn't believe that I was having this conversation in the middle of a graveyard that was being torn apart. How the hell did we get here? Where in the world, had this sick person who was responsible been treated or pressed so wrong to make them think this was a good past time? That this was a good way to get their rocks off? Where the hell did the body parts go, what the fuck was being done with them!?

"I can do that, Eric. I want this to be over with and I want answers as bad as you do. This is my life and livelihood and I feel like I have now let families down by not being able to provide actual peaceful rest to their loved ones' bodies. I want this as bad as you and as bad as this town."

We stopped walking and he turned toward me before speaking.

"Thank you, Laylin. Let's figure out who this sick motherfucker is."

Chapter Twenty-Three

I leaned against the single oak tree that stood at the beginning of the cemetery. I had gently walked over here and sat down after finishing my talk with Eric. He informed me that I could just relax for now and he would fill me in on how many more they found and then I could be walked through and shown in each one of their actualities.

It was already halfway through the day and Seth had almost all of the graves dug and the caskets pulled from below the earth. I scanned the cemetery back and forth, taking moments to pause and watch the work being done or the photographs being taken. I heard a few more shouts and saw more people wave over Eric, which only made me drop my head to observe the soft grass beneath me. I couldn't watch this anymore, I didn't even want to be a part of it anymore. The vomit feeling was now a permanent solution that seemed to be the only persisting reaction and emotion that was now attached between me and this situation. I never in my life would've thought that I would have had to imagine the feelings associated with seeing a disturbed body that had been tampered with and dismembered, let alone one that been completely pulled from its resting place. The feeling of total violation made me feel as though everyone could see through not only my clothes but my skin, leaving all my flaws and soul to the outside world to see and judge. This was a sacred place and one that was being put to trial continuously since the day we found the first horrific truth.

I heard the hoe shut done and I saw Seth sit back and put his feet on the lower half of the window. He was now done unburying all of his work that he had buried in the last few months and others work from years prior. By the look on his face, he needed his own quiet space and place to sit and digest. I didn't blame him, I liked Seth. Enjoyed his company but today, I didn't mind having this tree to myself away from the hustle and bustle of the crime scene.

I looked down at my watch and noticed that it was almost two o'clock in the afternoon. If everything was dug and they were able to fully move ahead with concluding how each casket looked, maybe Seth and I would be able to head home before it was super late. Go home and try to scrape clean the images and noises that accompanied today.

I stopped watching the little hand click away around the center of my watch and looked up to see Eric staring at me. He finally got the attention he was looking for and waved a fast hand across the air to wave me back over. I leaned against the tree and hauled myself up and straightened my clothes before making my trek over to where he stood by the last casket. It was that of the thirteen-year-old girl's and if all I could have from today was one answered prayer, I surely hoped to god that she would be the one that had been left alone and not disturbed.

My heart sank as the casket and inner contents came into view. It was empty and from the simple staining of plain ground water, I already knew the answer to the question that wanted to leave my mouth. She wasn't in there, never was for more than maybe a day after she was buried in the ground.

I felt a lump gather in my throat and tears threaten my eyes. Eric must've caught my reaction and reached up again to squeeze my shoulder. I could feel eyes from everyone on me but I couldn't dare to look at any of them. I knew what they wanted. They wanted an explanation, reasoning to this sickness that was travelling around what seemed to be the whole entire graveyard. She was just a girl, thirteen years old and not only lost her life but now had been ripped out of her casket that she had been put to rest so peacefully and soundly in, in the ground. I wanted the answers too, but I knew no one here could give them to me.

"So, what now?" I promoted as calm sounding as I possibly could maneuver myself to be. Eric cleared his throat before he replied and I felt his hand leave my arm.

"Same as before. Nothing really changes because we have not found any substantial evidence at this point. We have been sending evidence to the lab but haven't had any conclusive results back yet. Out of the nine caskets exhumed including the one that started all of this, there were five that had been completely robbed or dismembered. I will move forward with dealing with the media and the families with any questions they may have and you will follow with everything that we have previously discussed. With everything that has taken place, you and Seth are both free to be at home and on call until we need you or would like to talk to you. There isn't much more you guys can do for us here."

"Okay. And are we done for today as well? We can pack up and make our way home?"

"Yes. You are both able to leave."

"Okay." I could still feel eyes on me but only looked at Eric as I replied and stepped back to turn around and head over to retrieve Seth. I felt numb, like my legs were wobbly after being drugged or a really intense workout where they were now only noodles and doing the best they could to keep you from falling to the floor. Everything seemed muffled and far away from me too, I believe these were small signs of shock. What in the world had happened!? *What the fuck, Laylin, how could you let this happen!? How could you screw up so bad!?*

    I swallowed hard trying to drown out my inner voice that was doing nothing but taking rounds out of me. Seth noticed me coming and I waved my hand at him and pointed toward the truck. He quickly gathered his stuff and jumped out of the hoe with a slam of the door behind him. We both were ready to leave, just wouldn't look great to the cops to have two funeral workers running for the vehicle to get home and hide under the covers.

    As we got close to the vehicle, I asked Seth how he was feeling, he looked okay and had color in his face so he must've been doing a lot better than how I was feeling.

    "You're driving us home." I threw the keys at him and he barely caught them before stopping and looking at me with sincere concern.

    "You okay, Laylin?" I felt the tears start to try and come out at the question, but I couldn't let this kid see me weak, enough of the cop force already had.

    "No. Please drive me to my house and take this home if you want, or don't, whatever you want to do after you drop me off." I grabbed the door handle and climbed in with a swift slam of the door following closely behind me. I buckled my seatbelt and leaned my head against the headrest before closing my eyes and trying to imagine myself literally anywhere but here.

Chapter Twenty-Four

The clicking of my door closing and latching behind me seemed to be the sound that took a one-hundred-pound weight off of my shoulders. I felt like I could move a little easier and breathe a little bit better. I didn't really know how much all of this was affecting me until my home door shutting out the world, removed the unnecessary baggage that had climbed aboard and hung on for dear life all day long.

I walked over to grab a new bottle of wine. I should just kick this evening off with a nice smooth dependable friend that would know how to soothe the shaky hands and bring some peace and solitude to the madness. It didn't take me long and my glass was almost full to the brim. I put the bottle down and picked up my glass before turning around and heading to my couch and plopping down on the cushion, staring at my laptop lying on the coffee table in front of me. I took my first sip of wine while leaning my head against my arm that was propped up on the back of the couch. The silence of the room was beautiful and then a thought quietly crossed my mind.

I had cameras installed into the funeral home when it was first built and remodeled. They were always running and recording and putting away the recorded files into a locked system on my computer. We rarely ever used them or checked in on them because of the fact that they were installed to be used for break-ins or anything of suspicious nature. There rarely ever was and I could only think of the time when the alarm was bugging out and kept telling me that someone was entering and exiting at all hours of the night. Again, it turned out to be nothing but the alarm itself malfunctioning but all the files were always there and always stored and I was the only one with the password as well as the only one who was able to access the cameras. This was for obvious safety reasons and so no tampering was ever to be done with the tapes or cameras. Yes, I did trust my people who worked for me but people flipped like a switch sometimes, and you could never really be too sure. In retrospect, do I actually truly trust the people that I have working for me? Maybe not.

I scrunched my nose and took another sip of the blissful poison that I was drinking and filling my stomach with, awaiting the reaction of alcohol entering my bloodstream. I stared at my laptop as the questions and thoughts began to arise. If there was something there that was going on, this was all I needed. I could spend my night looking through them and then sending what I needed to Eric or calling him and having him look and watch for his own self to put the pieces together. These were my staff that I grew to care for, but something seriously screwed up was going on and this could be the key to the answers to it all and what all of us were searching for.

I leaned forward and clunked my glass down beside my laptop before picking it up and bringing it to rest on my lap. I opened it up and let it load for a second before I found my camera software and clicked on it to open it up. I'm glad I decided to incorporate it into my personal laptop too because this saved me from having to walk into my funeral home, where I didn't even want to be near right now.

The plots that were dug up were just recently buried within the last six months, so if there was anything wrong going on with one of my staff members it would be on here and I would be able to see it.

The cameras software opened up and the amount of files made my eyes automatically roll into the back of my head. By the looks of everything recorded and stored, I'd be here for hours and needing four bottles of wine. I let out a sigh and started to click through them one by one. I decided to fast forward and watch in hyper speed so that maybe things would go faster and I could put it down satisfied and try and enjoy the rest of my evening as best as I could.

I sunk down into my couch and leaned back into the cushions to get comfortable as I kept clicking and watching people walk around or move bodies throughout the halls. It only ever recorded movements or alarm notifications, never a full recording of absolutely nothing, which right now I was sure thankful for.

I moved my cursor down to click on the next recording when I noticed the time to be twelve thirty in the morning. I felt my forehead crinkle and looked closer to see if I was reading the time right. There should be no reasoning for the funeral home to be unalarmed and someone moving throughout it at that time. Even with intakes, we usually never met people in the middle of the night to accept bodies, it was always reasonably acceptable and time available to wait until first thing the following morning. The health department was the one that went to suicides or in-home deaths to pick up and store at the hospital until we were able to go and retrieve the bodies. So, there were never any bodies lying on a floor waiting until we got there in the morning.

I went to click on it but hesitated and hovered my mouse over it. What if this was it? What if I was about to become increasingly more disturbed and put out by watching someone I thought I knew, doing ungodly things to a dead body? The thought made me sit up and retrieve my glass to finish chugging it before opening the camera clip. With one last swallow I put the glass back down and repositioned myself into the corner of my couch.

Stop being a baby and click the damn file! My inner voice kicked into high gear. I clicked on the recording and took a breath as it opened up and started to play.

It was the main desk and reception area. Before too long, Ayda was walking into view and I could see a shadow of someone just behind the camera's view. She walked over to the desk and slowly slid her panties down and jumped on the desk before luring the shadowed someone over with her finger. My stomach lurched, what in the actual fuck!? I saw a guy walk into view and it didn't take long for me to realize who it was. Ayda picked up her legs and placed her feet on the desk and Seth gleefully got down onto his knees and took his position with his head between her thighs. I hit pause and slammed my hands over my face. What the fuck, guys!?

Of all the places to fuck each other, you come back to my funeral home to bang on the reception desk!? Okay, so it was true, I didn't have the slightest clue of everything that took place and went on in my own business. I hit play but hit the fastest speed I could to avoid the full in-depth porno that was being played out in front of me. After the gross fuck session was finished, the recording soon came to an end.

Okay, so I have a bunch of porn laid out in my camera recordings, awesome. Wonder how not to be awkward now knowing what Seth and Ayda are both working with. Ugh! The images wouldn't ever leave now and they repeatedly made me cringe.

    I scrolled down to see more videos of roughly the same time and wanted to not watch them, but what if in odds chance it wasn't the same nastiness I just witnessed? I mean, I was all for others getting their love on, but I was not into watching people I worked with do it. Reluctantly, I clicked on each one and fast forwarded every single one, losing my will to stay somewhat sober. I was almost halfway through the recordings when I noticed another one that was oddly timestamped. I leaned forward and placed my computer down on the couch. I stood up and rounded the couch to grab my opened bottle of wine and bring it back to the couch with me. I took another big swig before placing it beside my empty glass and picking up my laptop once again.

    This oddly timed recording was for three in the morning. I scrunched my nose and hit play. When the video came up, I realized that it was in my embalming room. I felt my stomach try to disconnect from my organs and leave my body.

    I leaned forward and grabbed my bottle to hold my hand through whatever I was about to witness. I picked it up and put it to my lips and started sipping when my eyes caught sight of some flashes moving just outside of camera view, along with hearing heavy shuffles and scuffs coming from my speakers. When I looked down, I could see there was now a corpse being moved onto one of the embalming tables, a corpse that was from one of the plots that was exhumed today. I instantly slammed my bottle back down beside my glass and sat straight upwards staring intently at my screen. Why was this body being embalmed so early in the morning? I didn't remember her being a special case or her body needing to be done quicker than most.

There were a few more noises and heavy breathing before a man came into view and situated himself right beside the body on the table. His features seemed familiar, but it was hard to make out at first. I felt my heart drop and a wave of puke wash over me before I could even debate running to the toilet or not. A gasp left my mouth as my jaw hit the floor, what the fuck was happening!?

Chapter Twenty-Five

My laptop was now sitting open on the coffee table while I leaned against my kitchen island bracing myself as my body shook. What I had just witnessed on that screen was something not even the movies could put on to act out. It was sickening, hellish and mighty disturbing. In fact, I believed this is what the dictionary meant when it spelt out and described the word disturbed.

It didn't take me long to recognize the man in the video, Gregory was indeed my embalmer, which made it all the more sickening to me. He had a wife and young kids, hell, he was an end of life care worker. People trusted within him to provide their deceased loved ones with nothing but the utmost respect and decency. He gave much more of a vigorous and creepily thorough explanation of embalming and cleaning up a corpse.

I walked over to grab my phone and find Eric's business card to call his cell. He may find it unprofessional to have to come over, but I had been drinking and no way was I going to explain over the phone what was happening or going on or what I had just witnessed.

I grabbed my phone and started to dial when I stopped typing numbers and shook my head.

"What am I doing right now!?" My voice was shrill as it came out. Projecting my outburst to my furniture because that was the only presence of anything else being around to hear me. I couldn't rat him out like this. Today was the first actual day of the investigation and if today was the day I conveniently found these videos, maybe I would be accused of helping or being a witness or accomplice or whatever the hell they wanted to place me as. I didn't do shit and I wasn't about to go down for some fucked up shit buddy had that helped him get his rocks off. How would that look to anyone? That I could feel the pressure of the investigation so I found a way to turn someone in? Nah, I wasn't about that and I sure as shit wasn't going down for some twisted individual who was caught on camera using some female's corpses hand to jerk his meat on my camera.

I needed to find a way to do this but to do it cautiously and so that I and my funeral home wouldn't be caught in the crossfire. He is my employee, how could I have not noticed someone or something like this going on!? People are screened for being necrophiliacs before they are even allowed into school for this type of work, but I guess anyone can hide whatever skeletons they wanted in their closet.

I placed my phone back down on the island and sat down on one of my bar stools and took a deep breath. Now I had to find a way to explain that one of my most valued and trusted employees that did beautiful work, was a corpse fucker. Even if it wasn't him that was tampering with the bodies after being put into the ground, it sure wasn't looking good for him now being a necrophiliac.

Chapter Twenty-Six

I paced back and forth up my kitchen with my bottle of wine. I had one swig left and I would be going onto my next bottle, which I damn sure needed right now. I couldn't exactly see the clock and didn't know how long I'd been pacing but it was something rather than sitting in the absorbing feelings of panic, anxiety ridden disturbance followed by harsh blows of nausea and clammy sweat soaked skin.

What the hell was I going to do? I had to do something, I couldn't just stay at home drinking and pacing all night long. What if Eric called me and said that they found a body or piece of a body that had been dismembered? What the hell would I do then? I couldn't keep what I had just witnessed under wraps when the whole town focus was on me and my funeral home and the missing corpses that were supposed to be sealed in the ground.

I walked back over to my phone, finished the last sip of wine and placed the empty bottle on my counter. I took a quick breath and picked it up to start dialing numbers in. As soon as I hit call, the phone started ringing. I nervously began to chew on my nails awaiting the other end to pick up.

"Hello?" Seth's tired voice croaked through the phone. I looked back over to my stove to realize that it was already almost two in the morning.

"Seth, it's Laylin. Did you take the work truck home with you?" My words were coming out sporadic and fast.

"Yeah, I did. It's two in the morning, did they find something else?" I heard a yawn come through the phone as he finished his question.

"Something like that. I need you to get dressed and come pick me up. Be at my house no later than two thirty." I hung up my phone and put it down before he could refuse or ask any more questions.

I walked down my hallway to my bedroom to throw on clothes and brush my teeth. I threw on fresh deodorant and got dressed. Hopefully, the toothpaste would mask some of the booze smell but at this moment, I had a driver so I wouldn't be participating in any illegal activities so far.

I gargled the water and spit it down the drain as I reached up and shut the tap off and wiped my mouth with my hand towel. I took one last look in the mirror and turned to head to the front door to slide my boots on. I heard the crunching of the gravel under truck tires pulling into my driveway and knew that Seth had arrived right on time. I ran back to my counter to grab my stuff and quickly fled back to the door, shutting the lights off as I was shutting the door all in one swift motion.

The night was cool and I could tell that fall was coming soon. It was still nice but there was that coolness that sliced through the air that would leave your skin cool with a slight chill to remind you of its kiss across your body. I grabbed the door handle and opened the door and climbed into the passenger seat quickly while shutting it behind me. Seth sat staring at me as though he was waiting for an explanation as to why I had drug him out of his bed without anything but a timeline.

"You need to take me to the funeral home. I need you to park in the farthest lot and shut the lights off as we come into the parking lot." It looked as though he wanted to laugh or cry, I wasn't exactly sure.

"What? You drag me out of bed to come get you at two thirty in the morning and that's all you say? To turn into sketchy people driving to the funeral home, to do what exactly? Did something happen?"

I felt the wine coursing through my veins and a small balled temper flaring onto my tongue. The outcome was probably going to be less than favorable but hey what more did I have to lose? So, I decided to let the Laylin led by red wine lead the reply to Seth.

"You are going to do exactly what I ask of you because you've been screwing Ayda in my front desk reception area for months and I can have your ass canned without any blink of an eye from me in the next few seconds that you decide to try and be smart. Your sex moves didn't impress me and furthermore, I don't have time for you guys' porn soap opera you got playing around. Now shut the hole in your face and drive the damn truck to the funeral home, as sketchy as you possibly can fucking be." I looked at Seth to see his face was turning pale paired with some red flush across his cheeks. Obviously, he had forgotten about the cameras we never used.

He didn't say another word and then turned back forward while putting the Tahoe into gear and steering us in the direction of the funeral home. I sat watching the light posts go by and for the first time in days my mind sat quiet. Nothing was popping around or freaking out and the tranquility of it, along with the heated leather seat that now hugged my body, made me want to lay my seat back and close my eyes.

My camera alert went off on my phone and it pulled me from my relax state. I had a feeling he would be using the time of the funeral home being shut down to manipulate and fondle bodies and my little hunch turned out to be true. Turning on my camera alerts let me stay with the most recent recordings and allow me to know exactly which cameras were going off and where Gregory was and what he was doing before I got there. I opened the recording to see the front entry door had been disarmed and opened at exactly three a.m. We were only twenty more minutes away and I knew the session I was about to disrupt was going to take two hours roughly start to finish, at least the last videos I watched of it all, usually all seemed to fall into that time frame.

Seth peered at me quickly before looking down at my phone. I had never had the app on my phone before so the new alarm would be a new sound notification to him too. I felt the air between us start to get heavy and tense. I knew he wanted to ask more questions as he was wondering what the hell was going on, but I couldn't give him an answer. I wasn't quite exactly sure what I was doing myself yet. I was just kind of winging it and hoping something good was bound to come out of it. I saw the lights flip off and felt the truck slow down. Man, time seemed so screwed up lately, either way too fast or way too slow. I undid my seatbelt and turned around to face Seth.

"I need you to stay here. Unless I call you or the alarm starts going off like crazy like there's an intruder, I need you to stay here, with the truck like this, just as everything is right now. Can you do that for me?" Seth nodded and then quietly watched me fumble with my phone to silent it and grab the handle to climb out of the Tahoe.

"I mean it, Seth." I stood on the ground while still holding the door open.

"I know, Laylin, I understand." I nodded my head and slowly shut the door until I heard the latch grab and I turned to start heading toward the side door. I was going to use this door, it would make less of a click as the bolts unlocked and I walked in. I reached the handle and took out my key fob to let me in. I took a small sigh as I held the handle and let it out slowly and evenly as the key fob lit up and I opened the door. I took a few steps to get inside and turned around to gently close the door behind me. It closed quietly and I stood holding my breath, waiting to hear if anything was changing or if someone's footsteps were going to start.

I listened for what felt like forever before I turned around to see the lights on in the embalming room. I started walking as quietly and slowly as I could be. This was it. What in the actual fuck was I thinking?

Chapter Twenty-Seven

Every muscle in my body was tense and it felt as though cold water was rushing through every one of my veins rather than the warm blood that was supposed to be occupying them.

What the hell was I doing? I didn't know what Gregory was capable of. I thought I knew this man but turns out I knew absolutely nothing about him. He had a sick and twisted nature and there was a part of his ticker that got stuck, thrown out an airplane window and blown apart in the turbine. There were just some parts of people that really needed to be there, just so they didn't dive so far off of the edge.

I was being as quiet as I possibly could but trying to breathe as evenly and deep as I could so that I wouldn't pass out before I reached the swinging doors that I was aiming for. The amount of adrenaline rushing through my body made it almost impossible to hear anything but the heartbeat in my ears and my own wavering shaky breaths. I could hear some rustling and then I could hear some faint moans coming through the cracks of the doors into the embalming room. My stomach churned and I thought I was going to puke in my hallway up against the wall.

Snap out of it! This is it! You need to boss up and walk in there and take ahold of this situation, Seth is outside, you're not alone here. The voice in my head was sure trying but damn I felt alone and about to confronted by a real life-sized nightmare that I only ever wanted to hear about in books or on TV.

I came to the doors and gently placed my hand on the door and pushed it open while I followed my hand through and into the embalming room. Gregory's back was toward me but I could see he was naked and thrusting with his head slightly titled back with slow moans leaving his mouth. A few cusses left his lips in small hisses and whispers and I felt even more uncomfortable while all the hair stood up on my body. I angled my head to see he had a corpse's head angled toward himself and its mouth propped open. He was empowering himself into a dead woman's mouth and gently holding the back of the body's head to stabilize everything.

I couldn't even fathom what the hell to say to break up the scene but I couldn't just stand here and watch it.

"What are you doing!?"

He almost slipped and fell down as my words left my mouth. He fumbled on the ground to try and stand and conceal himself. He looked shocked, then angry, and then embarrassed. We stood staring at each other for what seemed like hours and I glancing over toward the body on the table a few times.

"What the fuck, Gregory?" He looked down at himself now cupped between his hands and then back to the corpse on the embalming table. He looked almost sick himself, but I felt as though it was from being caught rather than the act in itself.

"You're just going to stand there? You have nothing to say, no excuses, and no motions to take a stand for yourself?"

He gently hung his head and I started to see tears fall. I felt a surge of guilt come across me but quickly shoved it away as I was not the one to be feeling guilty here.

"I'm so sorry, Laylin." He reached up with one hand to wipe his face and when he was done, grasped both hands back over himself. I looked around and saw a draping sheet lying a short distance away. I walked over and tossed it over him so he could wrap it around his waist. He caught it and quickly covered himself and tied it in a knot and then covered his face with his hands in shame as I stood staring at the whole scene playing out in front of my eyes.

"Sorry? You're sorry to me? How about to the body you're sexually mutilating, for what? Does your wife not suck you off enough at home, Gregory? Does the fucked-up porn that drives society just not do it enough for you? There are videos of all sorts, hell, you can jerk off to comic videos with a flesh light, but this!? This is beyond indifferent." I heard the sobs starting to come out now and I didn't know what to do. Before I could continue on with my words, he reached over and grabbed a scalpel off the instrument table and held it to his neck. My hands both shot up instantly in the surrender position.

"Stop, put the scalpel back down on the table, Gregory." My words stern but without a punishable tone. I wanted this situation to remain as calm as it possibly could.

"Why? No one would accept me this way, hell, I don't even accept myself, it's just my brain. My brain never stops, it tells me all the ways to be with bodies, they don't move or complain or deny. They take it always and willingly. There's no deviation or stalling. It's always here willing and waiting and then they are buried and no one says a word or punishes me." The tears were in a steady stream and I could see a small trail of blood coming from under the scalpel as he pushed a little harder into his skin with each one of his confessing words.

"Because your people, the people that love you, will want to help you. Help you work through this, be there for you. There are people to help you, help you portray this in a positive way. Help you overcome and harness your needs and desires into something that doesn't deem you as unacceptable in this society. We all have our quirks, but this doesn't have to define who you are. You can get help, I know you can. I have contacts, I can help you." My pleas were beginning to sound desperate and I could feel my heartbeat in my ears once again. I couldn't have a man slice his carotid artery in my embalming room that would make all of this a thousand times worse than it already was.

Gregory tightened his grip on the scalpel and started to push harder and the blood started to thicken and pool in his collarbone groove before making a trail down his chest.

"Please, Gregory. Let me help you. I was just caught off guard, this doesn't define you. I still see you; still see who I know you to be. Please let me take you to the hospital. Seth is outside and he can drive us both in and I will get you the help you need and this can stay between you and I and the doctors we see." I stood almost holding my breath and waiting for the tension in the air to lessen and for Gregory to drop the scalpel on the ground and come with me. I dropped my hands slowly and started to take a few small steps toward him. I placed my right hand out and motioned him to place the soon-to-be suicide weapon into the palm of my hand. I felt the cool steel gently land in my hand then backed up and threw it across the room hoping for it to land somewhere unrecognizable for the time being.

"Will you come with me?" Gregory slowly nodded and his sobs grew bigger and more intense. I could now see his clothes were by the door that I had walked through prior to the whole unbecoming of the situation. We headed toward it and he bent down to pick up only his shirt and slid it over his head. We made a quick exit out of the side door and headed toward the

Tahoe. I could see Seth's eyes grow huge and I hoped to god he would keep his questions to himself and his mouth shut. I heard the unlock as we reached the back door and I grabbed the handle to open it up and let Gregory climb into the backseat. I shut the door as he planted himself in the middle and hung his head toward the floorboards. I grabbed the passenger door handle and climbed back in beside Seth.

"Take us to the emergency room please, right now." Seth looked forward and threw the truck into gear and started off toward the hospital. I looked in the rear-view mirror to see Gregory's head still hanging in defeat and self-pity. This was it, we were so close and he could be put into safety away from my funeral home, the dead bodies temporarily occupying it and himself.

We made it to the hospital in less than ten minutes. Seth made the last turn and the emergency room sign lit up the inside of the cab. I took a small breath and grabbed my stuff ready to exit as soon as the wheels came to a stop on the pavement. The truck slowed and came to a jerky stop; I hopped out and went to the back to help Gregory out. He willingly climbed out and I looked back into the truck toward Seth, who was now watching our every move.

"Wait here and I'll be right back." I slammed the door and shuffled us both into the ER. I heard a small amount of gasps as the people waiting to be seen noticed the blood running down Gregory's neck. I ignored the sounds and stares and flagged down the triage nurse at the counter. She hurriedly rushed over with worry strewn across her face.

"I need you to get me Dr. Clyff right now and put this man into a private room while we wait. No objects of any kind and a clean gown." The nurse quickly nodded before grabbing

Gregory's hand and elbow and leading him out of the main focus of the waiting room and down a hallway to his own room while waiting to be seen by the doctor.

I turned and started to head back outside, ignoring all the looks from bystanders as the shock of what they just saw was still wearing off. I reached the Tahoe and opened the passenger door and looked in at Seth.

"I need you to go back to the funeral home. There's a body on the embalming table, I need you to place it back in the fridge and lock up and set the alarm. I will go and finish the embalming process in the morning when I'm finished here. You then park this at the funeral home and bring me back my personal vehicle. When you get here, park it and leave my keys on top of my back tire, out of sight as best as possible and lock it. Then find yourself a ride home, don't care how you get there but get there." He looked as if he just saw a ghost. I was turning to close the door when his words stopped me.

"What the fuck is going on, Laylin?"

"Everything is fine, Seth. Just go do what I said please and I'll call you if I need anything more or if the police do. Keep this to yourself. If anyone asks you, you slept all night long." I shut the door as I turned around to head back into the hospital.

Chapter Twenty-Eight

As I walked through the doors, I took my phone out and dialed Eric's number. He picked up after the second ring and his voice sounded rough and tired.

"Get dressed and meet me at the hospital in the psych ward, I'll be with Dr. Clyff." I hung up as soon as I was done with my statement. I had no time for hesitations or questions. He was chief of police, he understood urgency when he heard it and it was definitely there entangled into my words.

I stopped at the nurse's desk to ask the same triage nurse which room Gregory was now occupying. She pointed me in the direction of the last examination room and explained Dr. Clyff was already down with him, but I could carry on in without having to wait or sign in. I thanked her briefly before making my way down the hallway. I knocked on the door twice when I reached it before turning the handle and pushing the door open.

"Laylin, nice to see you." I shut the door behind me and walked over to the chair placed against the wall and took a seat.

"Dr. Clyff, you as well." I looked toward Gregory who had seemed to totally disassociate from himself now and become a soulless body puppet sitting on the examination bed.

"I was just telling Gregory that I will get his neck all stitched up, a shot of antibiotics and his room is being made up on the top floor for his stay." I nodded and continued to look at Gregory before replying back to Dr. Clyff. I figured at least a flicker of emotion would cross his face but nothing changed. He was a goner, completely detached creating a trauma surface to cover up for everything that just took place. He had become a human zombie.

"All sounds good, thank you, Dr. Clyff." Dr. Clyff was a smug man, he wasn't one of my favorites but him and I went way back and he always did me favors and I did favors in return. He tried to ensure the sexual kind but that was never one that I welcomed or even rattled back and forth with him like it was even an option.

He grabbed some materials and started to suture the open cut that was on Gregory's neck. It didn't take him long to stitch and bandage him up. By the looks of where I was sitting, it was eight stitches and some Steri strips covered over with a clean bandage. He discarded all of his tools and then threw his gloves into the garbage before stepping back and looking at me. I raised my eyebrows in reply and he smirked before turning back to look at Gregory.

"Okay, sir, you're all stitched up and I'll come remove those stitches in a few days. Let's get you upstairs and settled for the rest of the night, try and get you some sleep. By the sounds of everything, it's been a long night." Gregory slumped off the bed and we all shuffled out of the room behind Dr. Clyff. Gregory following closely behind and then me third in row behind him. We reached the elevator and we all stepped in when the doors opened, nobody saying a word. There wasn't anything for us to say. Everyone knew what was happening and taking place, as well as Clyff and I had been a part of many people's admissions into their grippy sock vacations.

The ding of the elevator along with the swell move of the doors sliding open and we all piled out and continued to room thirty-four which was just freshly cleaned and made up. The rooms on the psych floor were almost hotel standards and sometimes on my rough days I debated checking myself in and out of reality. I never found any shame in psych wards and actually found the people who came here to be brave enough to face their demons they tried to deny and hide down beneath the shadows.

    I watched Gregory walk in and sit down on his bed and I turned around to step out into the hallway. I heard Clyff say a few words to him and then a few nurses walked into his room and Clyff exited closing the door behind him.

Chapter Twenty-Nine

"Why did you bring him here, Laylin? I thought this shit was going to stay out of my hospital."

I felt insulted. After so many years and he still thought he could speak to me as though he was above me.

"This shit isn't supposed to be in my funeral home, but here it is central fucking station of the spotlight. Eric's had to play top dog role so that hasn't helped. Why the hell are your guys sending family trinkets to the remaining living family? Who the fuck did that!?"

Clyff stepped back and leaned against the wall, remembering to lower his tone. I heard footsteps and looked up to see Eric approaching us with Dr. Ava Knowle by his side. She was the known best psychiatrist in the country, so it wasn't a shock for her to show up to assess and take over. Ava knew the dark side of the world but chose to stay as blind as she possibly could to it all and make an honest name and living for herself. I didn't agree but respected her choice and was awed at her success and impact she had in the world.

"Ava briefly filled me in, but what exactly happened?" Eric's question made Clyff lay his head back against the wall.

"Ava." I shot a simple nod toward her.

"Laylin. Nice to see you." She stopped in front of me, forming a messy circle between the four of us.

"Gregory was fucking corpses in the embalming room. I have the camera specs. He tried to slit his throat so I brought him here. Seth drove us here but he knows nothing and is bringing my truck back so that I can leave. I'll forward you the videos, Eric, and you can do what you need to with them. Someone had to go down for this bullshit. Our deal was, this stays off the radar. The selling of bodies and dismembering is fine as long as my funeral home and name stay out of it and look where the hell we are at right now. Both of you should give your damn heads a shake. Find out who the fuck is sending trinkets from bodies to their family members and put them in the fucking ground or the river, I simply don't care. Don't let it happen again." They both stood staring at me knowing I was done messing around and lying low like the boss I normally was. I heard Ava clear her throat and it brought my attention back to her.

"Well, I will just excuse myself now. Everything regarding Gregory is done with you all now, other than the prosecution for whatever you all have going on. Thank you for the call, Dr. Clyff. Eric, Laylin."

"Ava." She turned and entered into Gregory's room, shutting the door behind her. I turned my attention back to the two men standing in the hallway with me.

"Get it done, gentleman, so we can get these caskets put back into the ground and get back to normal business as usual. If y'alls workers can't figure it out, they can be shoved into an empty casket and buried in the ground." I turned and started heading back toward the elevator to head to my truck. It had been close to a few hours and Seth would have been back and gone already. It was now nearing the hours of daylight and I could feel the exhaustion starting to set in.

Chapter Thirty

I pressed the elevator button and as I watched the light flash over the floor numbers my mind began to go through the last few days events that lead me up to here.

This was my business, it was strictly to be dealt with beyond my own eye sight and due diligence of retrieving bodies or only parts. There were men paid for that, highly paid. It was the typical, "Oh, Laylin, these new guys are great and good to the core to be trusted with this business." Now, I had families digging up bodies because they started to play their own sick games of sending family broaches back through the mail. I leaned my head against the wall for my last few seconds of the elevator ride and pinched the bridge of my nose.

My wine hangover was now kicking in and the soberness that brought it on faster was wailing a wicked headache between my temples. The elevator dinged and I walked out toward the front doors that lead out to the parking lot. The nurses gave a seldom goodbye and I nodded without missing a step on my way out. Everyone here was so terrified of me. The ones who knew anyways. I was never the one to beat, abuse, or kill anyone. There were paid men for that too. They all did exactly what I instructed though, so they would stay upright and breathing with nice paychecks rather than not breathing and placed in an unmarked grave underneath our feet. Being the funeral home owner made things like that so simple, that it was almost easier than learning how to park a car after driving for the first time.

The sunshine of a new day hit my face and I wanted to take it and drive home to sleep and shower off the blood and grossness that I felt. I rarely ever had to personally handle this part of my business and when I did, it exhausted me emotionally. Men seemed to be so incapable of keeping things how they were supposed to be. There was always a slip because the mentality of "Bros before Hoes" had fallen through the cracks a long time ago, but they never seemed to catch on or figure it out. Anyone could be a sneaky rat that didn't know how to keep their mouths shut and then we had to come down to picking one sore sucker to pay for a crime he didn't do, to get the Ferris wheel back spinning to its proper function and axis point.

Unfortunately, Gregory was the sore sucker in this story. It all just got too big and too focused. There were news teams from all over and everything was pointed toward us. We needed a deterred escape and he was the way to go. He was a genuine guy but had a fucked up side which made him the perfect pick. Eric would make sure that he got a full luxury prison ride and safe from other inmates. And Ava would make sure he made it to his final housing rest at her facility. When he was all finished and when he got out, his life would be hell. People would shame him until he moved away or succeeded with slitting his throat.

My boots thudded on the pavement with certainty and I continued on to my truck. I found my keys on the back tire where I told Seth to leave them and quickly unlocked it and hopped into the driver's seat. I sat back and leaned against my seat and turned some music on after starting the engine. I needed a good tune to revamp my day so I could get back to the funeral home and finish embalming the corpse Gregory was having his way with.

I put my truck into gear and started to drive out of the hospital parking lot and back toward the funeral home. What a beautiful day it was going to be today. I finally felt the relief from the previous days of stress wash through me and my shoulders seemed to relax.

See when I was younger and just freshly graduated from funeral services school, I had an intriguingly handsome man approach me one day after work. We small talked for a bit before he explained that he thought I would be perfect for this kind of work. Before the onset of smaller in-depth details, he ensured me to humor him.

Once he was done with some explicit explanation, I was fully disturbed, disgusted but curious. He left me with his number and told me to sit with it. I called him a few days later needing to hear his voice take me over every letter slowly and intricately to fully let it sink in and absorb into my brain. I always agreed that if I started, I would only do it to get ahead and then I would stop and pull out of it but the money and the thrill of power accompanied by the job position, was a high, that even ecstasy couldn't achieve for me.

The mystery of the whole disturbance was always quite simple. You see, I just sell the bodies and parts to the higher up men and women of this world. The riches, the top notches. They have their obsessions and disturbing traits but I never judge because selling a woman's head put seven hundred and fifty thousand dollars into my bank account and all I had to do was click confirm and get the order done with. I heard from a friend that that head is now the beaming party attraction for that man's den and he's the one that runs part of this country.

See everyone has the ability to be sick and twisted and money is what drives us all. You could be anyone and if someone offered you two million dollars deposited directly into your bank account, you'd pull a corpse from the ground and hand it to two men in black suits to take to their boss so he could make a full like sex doll.

What happens beyond my ordered confirmed and money transferred is nothing to me. I don't care but when I become the spotlight then there's a problem. Especially when there are new guys intentionally fucking it up. Then they will become new ornaments of my graveyard. It's really a plain and functionally laid out simplistic process.

See what people don't understand is the sickness that runs through the world every day. Any smiley face can be the game changer of life and death within a second. I can make one go away to benefit me greater by expanding more financials into my bank account. You either wake up and open your eyes to what's happening and become a part of it or you bury your head in the sand and become oblivious.

There are only two sides, never a middle meridian to jump onto and play both fields. The world is sick; you just had to decide whether or not you were going to pay attention to it.

I had a few more minutes to the funeral home and I felt a smile creep across my lips for the first time in days. It felt good to get everything back in order and to be done with all of this bullshit. In this world, it was the definition of successful to be a woman in power of a world that was run entirely on money, deceit, and pleasure.